Soldier
Boy

BRIAN BURKS

Soldier Boy

HARCOURT BRACE & COMPANY

San Diego　　New York　　London

TO LYNN

Copyright © 1997 by Brian Burks

Requests for permission to make copies of any part
of the work should be mailed to: Permissions Department,
Harcourt Brace & Company, 6277 Sea Harbor Drive,
Orlando, Florida 32887-6777.

Library of Congress Cataloging-in-Publication Data
Burks, Brian.
Soldier boy / Brian Burks.
p.   cm.
Includes bibliographical references (p. 152).
Summary: A boy who grew up in the slums of late nineteenth-
century Chicago runs away, joins the cavalry, and fights with
General Custer in the Battle of Little Bighorn.
ISBN 0-15-201218-4
ISBN 0-15-201219-2 pb
1. Custer, George Armstrong, 1839–1876—Juvenile fiction.
[1. Custer, George Armstrong, 1839–1876—Fiction.
2. Frontier and pioneer life—Fiction.]
I. Title.
PZ7.B9235So   1997
[Fic]—dc20   96-30289

Text set in Dante
Designed by Linda Lockowitz
First edition
F E D C B A
F E D C B A (pb)

Printed in Hong Kong

Author's Note

LITTLE HAS BEEN written about the surprisingly large number of frontier army recruits who were under the legal age of enlistment during the period of the Indian wars: 1865–1890. Having only the slightest notion of what life in the army was like, these young men enlisted for a variety of reasons. Some wanted to escape parental authority, while others sought relief from backbreaking farmwork. The glittering words of a recruiter, the glamour associated with the wearing of a uniform, and the

opportunity for travel and adventure drew
many.

But to most, the army was simply a living. Jobs were scarce, especially for the
unskilled and illiterate. Compared to the
meager fifty-cents pay for a sixteen-hour
day, when work could be found, army
benefits were very attractive.

Whatever their reasons for lying about
their age and joining the army, few recruits
found frontier military life what they had
imagined. Veteran soldiers, bored from the
monotonous routine, looked upon the arrival of green company replacements as a
welcome diversion. New enlistees were
tested by relentless hazing. Those who en-
dured it with good humor were eventually
accepted as members of the company.
Those who didn't were scorned and sometimes even forced to desert.

Army discipline was strict, and the sergeants in charge were chosen for their
toughness. The smallest infraction of the
rules frequently resulted in severe, sometimes illegal punishment.

Nearly all Indian-wars recruits were required to go out into the field on campaign duty against what the government viewed as hostile Indian tribes. Most new recruits had no idea what to expect and were ill-equipped and poorly trained. Many were sent into battle having never practiced riding a horse or shooting a gun.

Based on thorough historical research, the places, characters, and events in *Soldier Boy* depict frontier army life that is typical and authentic for the period.

The Kid

^

JOHNNY "THE KID" McBane ducked a deadly blow aimed at his left temple and came up with a short, powerful jab to the ribs of his older, much larger opponent.

The bearded man grunted, and Johnny hit him again in the same place, then landed a right hook to the man's chin that popped like a small-caliber gunshot. The crowd in the Chicago gambling house known as The Store went wild, either cheering or moaning for the fighter upon whom they had placed their bets. Johnny's opponent staggered backward in astonishment and wiped at the blood oozing from his mouth.

The Kid just stood there, watching. That last punch had caused intense pain in his right hand, and he hoped one of his knuckles wasn't broken.

Though he'd had little formal training as a boxer, the Kid knew better than to waste these precious seconds. Dozens of fights had taught him better. Now was the time to press his opponent, to land one blow after another until his arms turned to jelly and felt too heavy to lift—or his adversary fell.

Still, he hesitated. Suddenly his shoulders were gripped tightly from behind, and a grating voice whispered in his ear. "What are you doin', Kid? I told you to lose this fight. Do it or you're finished. There's too much at stake. You cross me now and you won't live to see tomorrow."

Enraged, Johnny jerked away from the hands that held him. Bare-knuckle boxing was the one thing—the only thing—he had found he was good at. This fight could be his eleventh straight victory. He was finally more than just a broom-pushing, spittoon-cleaning saloon boy, the illegitimate son of a dead Irish prostitute. He was *somebody*.

There were thirty gambling houses on Clark, Dearborn State, and Randolph Streets, and he was known in all of them. Men he'd never seen before stopped him on the street, slapped his back, and shook his hand. Harlots who made their living in the small, dingy back rooms of saloons and brothels offered him their quarters and their food. He wasn't exactly like royalty yet, but if he could keep winning, it wouldn't be long.

The crowd roared as the bearded man regained his composure and started toward the center of the spectator-formed ring. Johnny watched him while his thoughts raced. He knew that his fight promoter and manager, Julian Dean, was serious about his whispered threat. Thousands of dollars had been bet on this bout, and the small-time thief and ex-pickpocket wouldn't hesitate to use his countless connections to see that Johnny "the Kid" McBane was never seen or heard from again.

No one would really care. Not in the vice districts of Chicago in 1876, where murders and mysterious disappearances were an everyday occurrence. By tomorrow night Dean would have another fighter in the ring, and the betting would begin anew.

Johnny raised his arms just in time to block a bone-jarring roundhouse to his middle. His opponent was furious and threw a series of punches so fast Johnny couldn't block them all. He hurt, and the longer his indecision kept him from either fighting back or slumping to the floor in defeat, the more he would suffer.

A blow to his forehead erased Johnny's thoughts. The smoke-filled room began to spin, and he felt himself falling when another blow sent him crashing to the floor.

Instinctively, while the crowd roared, Johnny struggled to rise to his feet. He made it to his knees and was shaking his head, trying to clear his blurred vision, when he heard some of the people in the crowd start to chant his name.

The chants grew louder, and in them

Johnny found strength. Whether he lived to see tomorrow or not, today, at this moment, he was somebody, and he couldn't let himself or his fans down. Warily he rose to his feet, expecting his opponent to meet him with a flurry of punches.

Instead, the cruel-looking man laughed and spoke to the crowd. "Look at the runt. He ain't even weaned yet. I better send him on home to his mama."

Someone shouted from the back of the room, "He's weaned enough to give you that fat lip!"

The man touched his swollen mouth. Then he raised his fists and rushed toward Johnny. He was angry and too sure of himself, and he left himself wide open.

Johnny met him with a solid right to the nose and a follow-up left to the belly.

Blood gushed from the man's nostrils as he swung wildly with both fists.

Johnny ducked and took a half step back. He feinted a left hook while throwing a right to the man's jaw. The punch was solid, and the man staggered backward, dropping his guard.

This time Johnny didn't hesitate. He threw a flood of punches until he felt his strength starting to fade. Sweat beaded Johnny's forehead and trickled into his eyes, stinging them. His arms grew heavier with each swing. He was beginning to wonder if his battered opponent would ever fall when, at last, the man collapsed in a heap on the floor.

Oblivious to the cheers and howls of the crowd, Johnny wiped the sweat out of his eyes with the back of his raw-knuckled, bloody hands and turned around, looking for Julian Dean. He didn't look long. Three house bouncers were coming toward him, and Dean was right behind them.

Someone handed Johnny his shirt, which he quickly put on while pushing his way through the crowd toward the bat-wing front doors. He had no regrets. He might be caught, but he didn't plan to make it easy. Dean and his thugs couldn't kill him if they couldn't find him.

A Cold Ride

AN ICY BREEZE struck Johnny's sweaty body as he ran out of The Store and into the dark night. He wished he'd had time to get his coat. Snow crunched beneath his feet, and his breath fogged thick in front of him.

Shouts came from behind. "There he is! Catch him. Don't let him get away."

The report of a gun ripped the night apart, and Johnny pushed himself faster, without looking back. He passed the street corner where he normally turned to go to his small room on the top story of Madame Rosenberie's boardinghouse.

He couldn't go there now. Dean would expect it. Within minutes, the man was sure to search the place and take the prize money hidden in the mattress. Except for a few old clothes and a new brown derby hat, there was nothing more to go back for.

Johnny continued to run, turning off onto one side street after another, until at last his lungs could take no more and he slowed to a walk. A light snow began to fall, visible only in the glow of the street lamps.

Johnny looked back for the first time since leaving The Store. The narrow street he was on was empty. For the moment, he was safe.

A plan formed in Johnny's mind as he walked on. A plan that frightened him, yet seemed to be the only solution to his predicament. He must leave Chicago, leave the only life he had ever known.

The thirty-six cents in his shirt pocket wouldn't last long, and if he stayed with any of his friends, he'd be putting their lives in danger. Although he knew the streets and alleys of the city as well as anyone, it would only be a matter of time until Dean found him. Yes, he had to leave town, at least for a while.

∧

As JOHNNY STOOD by a set of railroad tracks, the light of a slow-moving freight train came toward him out of the switchyard. His teeth chattered from the cold, and he pulled tighter around his neck the filthy blanket he had bought from a wino for five cents. He was lucky, he knew. The wait for a train could have been a long one.

The train crept closer, and Johnny moved back from the track, where the light from the locomotive could not find him. He watched the clouds of steam billow up from the engine's smokestack.

Johnny had never been on a train, never tried to hop a ride on one, but he'd heard stories from hobos and others who had. It didn't sound too difficult—unless you missed your jump and slid underneath. Then the wheels cut you in two.

"Just watch for a car with the doors open," the rail tramps had said, "and climb in."

The locomotive passed with a deafening roar, and Johnny stepped close to the long snake of cars rolling behind it, surprised at how fast they were traveling. It was impossible to tell which of the large, blurred shapes had their side doors open until they went by, which left no time to prepare for the jump.

Seven cars passed as the tension inside him grew. He'd already missed one car with its doors open, and there might not be another. If he failed to catch this freight, it might be daylight before the next train rolled out. Then he would have to wait until the cover of darkness to try again.

The cars were moving faster. Johnny slung the blanket over his shoulder and wrapped the end of it around his arm. A flatbed car appeared, loaded with something in the middle. Johnny started to run with it, hoping he wouldn't trip. The car began to pass him and he dived for the side.

He hit the edge on his stomach and groped wildly at the plank floor for anything to help him pull himself up. He was sliding backward, about to fall, when his fingers found a crack between the boards and he steadied his position.

Back and forth he swung his body, until finally he had enough momentum to swing aboard.

Johnny lay on his back, gasping. He had made it. Barely. How some of the older hobos he had listened to did it was beyond him, unless they slipped into a car before the train started to move.

Several minutes passed before Johnny was able to sit up and spread the blanket over his shoulders. He crept toward the large object in the center of the car. It was a tall wooden box covered by a canvas tarp. Probably some type of farm or mill machinery, he guessed.

His hands and ears ached from the cold, and he crawled behind the box, knowing it would help block the wind and snow. He found that the heavy tarp was larger than the box, so he untied two of the bottom ropes securing it and slid under the canvas, resting his back against the box.

It wasn't bad, he decided. Probably warmer than a drafty boxcar, and here he wasn't likely to be seen.

The flatcar vibrated and swayed gently from side to side as it rolled, and the wheels made a steady, rhythmic clicking each time they hit a rail union. Johnny wondered which direction the train was headed. Though he had never been out of Chicago, he had heard about other towns nearby. Omaha was to the west, and St. Louis to the south. St. Paul was somewhere, maybe north. It really didn't matter where he was going, so long as it was away from Dean and his men.

He thought about his ex–fight manager, about the first time he had met him. Johnny had been kneeling by the bar in the Silver Slipper saloon cleaning a brass spittoon when a tall man in a striped suit stepped up beside him and spit a long stream of tobacco juice that splattered heavily on the top of his head. The stranger laughed, and Johnny lost his temper—all of it. He stood and threw a flurry of punches that sent the man sprawling across the floor.

Julian Dean had been watching from a table nearby. He came up and handed Johnny a towel. "Lad," Dean said, "stick with me and you'll never have to clean spittoons again. You'll be rich. Famous. I've never seen anyone who can fight like you."

Dean had treated Johnny well at first, finding him a better place to live and offering him pointers to improve his boxing style. Later, when large amounts of prize money had begun to pour in and Johnny's fame had grown, Dean turned sullen, often reminding Johnny of all he had done for him. The relationship had been strained, and Johnny's refusal to lose the fight tonight was just the final step in ending it.

An uneasy feeling forced Johnny's earlier sureness away. Maybe he should have thrown the fight, as Dean had wanted. He would have been paid well. All he'd have had to do was go down and stay there. If he had done it, he would still have his room, his clothes—his money.

The memory of his name being chanted by the crowd washed over Johnny, and he knew he had done the only thing he could. His pride was still intact, and he was a winner. Dean couldn't take that away from him. Nobody could.

The clicking of the car wheels was soothing. Johnny lay down, making sure the tarp and blanket covered him, then curled up in a ball to keep warm.

Maybe being forced out of Chicago was the best thing after all. He had no relatives to miss. A whole world was out there, a world he knew nothing about. He would do all right. Everything was going to be fine.

Johnny "the Kid" McBane pulled the blanket over his face and fell asleep.

St. Louis

^

THE TRAIN STOPPED and Johnny awoke, surprised at how warm he was. He slowly raised the edge of the tarp, and daylight flooded in. Several inches of snow covered the railroad car bed, explaining the reason for his cozy quarters: The snow had formed a thick, insulating blanket over the tarp.

He started to rise to his knees, and pain shot through him. He had taken more of a pounding in last night's fight than he had realized, and his muscles were stiff and sore.

But the pain would go away in a few days, he knew. It always did.

Forcing himself up, he stuck his head out from under the tarp. Except for the sound of the idling locomotive, it was quiet. Nothing moved. He crawled out onto the open car bed and peered around the corner of the box. A city lay in the distance. Closer, another freight train moved across the path of the one he was on.

Johnny stood up beside the box, put his blanket over his shoulder, and stretched his legs. He thought it might be better to get off here and walk to town rather than ride in on the train and risk being discovered.

He crouched down at the car's edge. No one could be seen alongside the train in either direction, so he quickly slid down, landing on his feet in the soft, deep snow. He forced his aching body to run in the direction of a nearby grove of oak trees, half expecting to hear the shouts of a railroad man behind him.

The shouts didn't come, and Johnny reached the grove. He continued on at a walk, wondering what city he had come to.

Whatever happened here, he couldn't be any worse off than if he had stayed in Chicago. His stomach told him the first thing to do was spend part of the money in his shirt pocket on some food. Because he couldn't eat right before a fight, his last meal had been yesterday at noon.

It didn't take him long to reach the outskirts of the city. The place looked big, maybe every bit as big as Chicago. Smoke from hundreds of chimneys drifted lazily upward before disappearing into the overcast sky. He kept walking, keeping his route parallel to the railroad tracks. If the city was anything like Chicago, the main business district would not be too far from the depot.

Some time later he was walking along a busy street, peering into various store windows to see if they served food. He passed two that did, but they looked to be too high class for his clothes or his budget.

The looks of a small café on the corner finally pleased him, and he went in and sat down at the counter. A plump woman in a red-checked dress started to hand him a menu, but he waved it away. "Do you have soup, ma'am? I'd like all the soup and crackers ten cents will buy."

She smiled, an understanding look in her eyes. "I think it will buy just about all you can eat, if you'll settle for beef stew. You want a cup of coffee to go with it? It's free to all my customers."

"Thank you," Johnny said. As she turned, he stopped her. "Ma'am, what town is this?"

"Why, you're in St. Louis, honey. Where have you been?"

Johnny hesitated, then decided it wouldn't hurt to tell her. "Chicago."

"Well," she said as she moved a loose strand of gray hair from her forehead, "you're not far from home. You just sit tight while I go into the kitchen."

Johnny was halfway through his second bowl of stew when a clean-shaven, middle-aged man stepped in and dusted a few snowflakes off his neatly pressed blue uniform. He removed his odd-looking spiked helmet, nodded at Johnny, and sat down two stools away.

"Morning, Sergeant," the woman said. "How's the recruiting business today?"

"Slow." His expression was somber, then he half grinned. "You wouldn't want to sign up, would you? We could cut your hair and dress you up like a man. You could see the West for free, make good money while you're doing it, and get a pension when you're through."

She laughed, setting a cup of coffee on the counter in front of him. "It's that bad, huh?"

The man sighed. "Afraid so. Guess I'll just have a slice of pie. Doesn't matter what kind."

The West. Johnny had heard stories about it from the miners, trappers, and soldiers who frequented the saloons where he had worked. It was a vast place, with mountains so high they could not be climbed and valleys so wide it took a week or more to cross them.

There were parched deserts and seas of grassy plains where thousands of buffalo roamed. There were mountain men, cowboys, and heroes like Buffalo Bill and Wild Bill Hickok. And there were Indians.

Johnny had been told that any man could go there with nothing and make his fortune in gold, furs, or land. The West was a place—the last place—where a man could really be free.

Johnny glanced at the man's uniform. It triggered a memory from childhood—he had been watching a group of Union soldiers parade through Chicago at the close of the Civil War. People were gathered along the street, clapping and cheering. The soldiers' steps were brisk, and they held their heads high. They were proud men.

The army. The thought of joining the army had never occurred to Johnny before. But it did now as the recruiter's words ran through his mind: *See the West for free, make good money while you're doing it, and get a pension when you're through.*

It can't get any better than that, Johnny thought excitedly, shoveling in another spoonful of stew. And it would be a long time before it was safe for him to return to Chicago.

He swallowed and turned to the sergeant. "Excuse me, sir, but how much does the army pay?"

The recruiter's eyes gleamed. "Thirteen dollars a month, a place to stay, and all you can eat. A smart lad like you is sure to make corporal soon, and your pay will jump to seventeen dollars. Plus, in your third year, you get an extra dollar per month, two in your fourth, and three in the fifth.

"You get all that, a clothing allowance, and free transportation all over the West. To serve your country by joining the army is the finest thing any young man can do."

The recruiter set his fork down, and his eyes narrowed. "How old are you, son?"

Johnny didn't answer. He was busy running the figures through his mind. The pay was fair. The most he'd ever made working saloons was ten dollars a month, and out of that he'd had to pay for his own room and board. Of course, once the fight game started the pay was better, sometimes as much as twenty dollars a bout. But that was over, at least for now.

The soldier impatiently tapped his knuckles on the counter, breaking into Johnny's thoughts and bringing him back to the unanswered question. The problem was, he didn't *know* how old he was, nor how old he needed to be to join. He guessed his age at sixteen, but he could just as easily have been fifteen or seventeen.

He answered in the best way he could think of. "I'm old enough."

For a moment the recruiter's eyes and expression showed doubt, but then the lines in his face relaxed. "Maybe you are, at that." He reached for his coffee cup, took a long swallow, and stood. "My office is just around the corner, two doors down. When you're finished eating, come by and see me."

The woman stepped out of the kitchen. "You're through already, Sergeant? Don't you want some more coffee?"

"No, thanks," he said, picking up his spiked hat and gesturing at Johnny with it. "Put this lad's meal on my tab and give him a big piece of that blueberry pie for dessert. I'm leaving to get his paperwork ready. He's about to join the army."

"No, sir." Johnny dropped his spoon and stood. "I ... I mean I might, but I need some time to think on it."

"What's to think about? You're broke, aren't you?"

"Nearly," Johnny answered. "But I can find work around. I always have."

"Sure you can, but I'll bet it won't pay what I'm offering you, let alone the other benefits. You come on by my office and we'll get you fixed up. Why, by tonight you'll be at Jefferson Barracks awaiting your first assignment out west. It's a decision you'll never regret."

Johnny slowly sat back down. The recruiter was right. He probably couldn't find a job that paid as much as the army, and the idea of being a soldier and going west was exciting.

"I'll come by, but ... but just to talk a little more."

"That's fine. I'll answer all your questions, and you won't be able to think of a single reason why you shouldn't sign up today."

A Soldier

∧

JOHNNY MCBANE stood outside the army recruiting office, gazing at the American flag draped in the window. The sergeant had been right, he reflected. For the last half hour or so he had remained in the café eating pie and drinking coffee, trying to think of one good reason *not* to join the army—without success.

Instead he had come up with several reasons why he should, foremost of which was that he had nothing to lose. Besides, it wasn't every day a person got the opportunity to travel around the country for free.

He opened the door, and the sergeant stood up behind his desk. "Come in. Did you get filled up?"

"Sure did." Johnny smiled, then shut the door and walked to a chair in front of the desk. "I never ate so much in all my life. Thanks for buying it."

"Oh, it's nothing, nothing at all. Take a seat. I have a few questions I need to ask you. Just formalities, you know."

Johnny sat down, putting his folded blanket on the floor beside him while the sergeant settled into his chair and took a pen from the inkwell on his desk.

"First thing is, you just look a little younger than you really are. You're twenty-one years old, right?"

Johnny hesitated a moment, then nodded.

"Good. Don't forget that. Now, give me your full name."

"Johnny McBane."

"Spell the last for me."

Johnny looked down, silent.

"What's the matter?"

More silence.

The sergeant leaned back in his chair and it creaked loudly. "You can't read or write, can you?"

Johnny's voice was low. "I never went to school."

"Well, don't worry about it. There's been some talk about Congress establishing a minimum education requirement, but they haven't done it yet. What's your mother's and father's names?"

"My mother's name was Louise. She died when I was little. I don't know anything about my pa."

The recruiter wrote something on the paper. "How tall are you? What do you weigh?"

"I...I don't know." Johnny shrugged. "Maybe five feet eight or nine inches and a hundred and fifty pounds."

"Perfect. They'll get it exact when you take your physical at the recruit depot."

"Recruit depot?"

"Jefferson Barracks. It's only a few miles from here. Let me see now..." The sergeant continued to write. "Your complexion is fair, hair...brown, eyes"—he glanced at

Johnny—"light blue. Do you have any in-firmities?"

Silence.

"Do you have any ailments? Is there anything wrong with you, like your hearing or vision, bad teeth or flatfeet?"

"No."

"Do you have any habits? Tobacco or drinking?"

"No."

"Do you have a trade? Are you skilled at anything?"

"No . . . well, there's one thing. I can fight."

"What do you mean?"

"Prizefighting." Johnny's voice showed his enthusiasm. "Bare-knuckle boxing. I was pretty good at it."

"Why did you quit?"

"It's a long story. Things just didn't work out. But I didn't lose. I won my last fight."

"I see."

The sergeant took the paper off his desk and looked it over. "Looks like we've filled in all the squares. I put down that you wanted to enlist for three years. It's either three or five. That all right with you?"

Johnny nodded.

"Good then." He placed the paper on the desk in front of Johnny along with a pen. "Sign here." He pointed. "Just put an X or whatever mark you like."

Johnny picked up the pen. "After I sign, is that all there is to it?"

"Except for your oath of allegiance. After that I'll get you transportation to Jefferson Barracks. Tonight you'll sit down to your first meal in the army."

Johnny started to make a mark, then stopped. Something had been nagging at him, and he finally realized what it was. "When I told you how tall I thought I was and how much I weigh, you said that was perfect. Perfect for what?"

"The cavalry, son. I'm a cavalry recruiter. Your size is important because a government horse shouldn't have to carry more than two hundred and forty pounds. That weight includes you, your saddle, weapons, ammunition, blanket, and rations.

The cavalry won't take men who are too big."

"But...I've never been on a horse. I don't know anything about horses."

"Doesn't matter. You'll learn."

Jefferson Barracks

^

S TRIP."

Johnny glared at the doctor. He had no more than arrived at Jefferson Barracks when an unfriendly soldier with two stripes on his sleeve had hurriedly ushered him into the small room where he now stood.

For more than an hour he had been waiting for he knew not what, and finally a man wearing a white coat and round wire-rimmed glasses walked in and commanded him to take off his clothes. Johnny had never been to a doctor before, and the thought of letting the man examine his naked body did not appeal to him in the least.

The doctor slid his glasses further down his nose and peered over them. "Take off your clothes, Private. That is an order!"

Johnny did not move. The doctor turned to the door and put his hand on the knob. "I don't have time for this. All I want to do is look you over, make sure your chest is ample, your limbs work, and that you do not have any obvious tumors or old wounds.

"It won't take long. If you refuse, I'll have the guards take you to the bullring until you learn how to follow instructions."

The *bullring.* Johnny wondered what that was, but wasn't sure now was a good time to find out. He slowly started to unbutton his shirt. It wouldn't hurt to let the doctor have a look. There were probably going to be a lot of things about army life he wouldn't like, and he might as well get used to them.

Soon Johnny left the room with a piece of paper the doctor had handed him. The same soldier who had escorted him there rose from a bench in the hall and motioned for him to follow. They stepped out of the building into the dusk light and headed toward a small, square building with a tin roof.

"Where we going?" Johnny asked, not wanting to be surprised again.

"You'll find out," the soldier snorted.

Inside the building was a long counter. Another soldier, with three stripes on his sleeve, was behind it. "Give me the form."

Johnny handed it to him. The man left, returning in minutes with a tall bundle of clothes, which he tossed on the counter. Half of them fell to the floor at Johnny's feet.

"There's your first issue of clothes, bub. One navy blue wool sack coat, two pairs blue kersey trousers, two gray flannel shirts, two suits of underwear, one caped overcoat, one pair of boots, one belt, and one forage cap.

"You got your clothes, now get out of here."

It was all Johnny could do to control his temper. "How do you know they will fit?"

"They won't, never do, but they're as close as I've got to the size the doc wrote down. Now get 'em and get out."

Johnny bent down and picked up the clothes, fighting the urge to leap over the counter and punch the man. He stood up, gathered the remainder of the clothes from the counter, and followed his guide outside.

The next stop was a long, rectangular building with the light from several kerosene lamps shining through the windows. The soldier led him up the plank steps to the entrance and opened the door.

Twenty or more men in various stages of undress were standing, or sitting, or lying on their beds. The room grew quiet, all eyes glued to the newcomer. Johnny's guide stopped at the far end of the room and gestured to his right.

"This is your bunk. Put your clothes in this." He stepped on a wooden box at the foot of the bed. "Lights-out at nine-thirty. Reveille's at five-thirty in the mornin', mess at six. Any questions?"

Johnny set his clothes on the bed. He did not know enough about what he had gotten himself into to know what to ask, and everything was happening so fast his thoughts were jumbled. "When's supper?"

"You missed it." The soldier sneered, then turned sharply and left.

Johnny stood self-consciously, looking the barracks over. There were two rows of bunks, one on each side, a large potbellied stove in the center, and various articles hanging from pegs on the wall. One of the recruits standing closest to him, a wiry-looking red-haired youth who couldn't be much older than Johnny, stepped forward and thrust out his hand.

"My name's Frank, Frank Gann. My bunk's next to yours."

Johnny grinned. Frank's was the first friendly face he had seen since his arrival at the recruit depot. He shook the soldier's hand. "I'm Johnny McBane. Nice to meet you."

The other men turned their attention back to what they were doing before Johnny's entrance, and the room filled with noisy talk. Frank took one of Johnny's shirts off the bed. "I'll help put your clothes up if

you want. There's a certain way the sergeant wants 'em folded, and he'll throw 'em
ever'where in the morning if they're not
just right."

"Thanks," Johnny said, sitting on his
bunk and reaching for his new army-issue
boots. He inspected them carefully. The
construction was so poor he could hardly
tell the left foot from the right, and the
cheap, coarse leather was cracked in several
places.

"You won't like 'em," Frank said with a
smile. "The prisoners at Fort Leavenworth
make 'em out of reject leather, and they
don't much care how they turn out. If you
wear 'em in water and then keep 'em on
your feet a day or two, they'll fit better."

Johnny laid the boots to the side and
watched his newfound friend's large, cal-
lused hands carefully fold another shirt.
Frank was somewhat thinner than Johnny,
but taller, and his sun-lined, freckled face
showed a life spent outdoors.

"Where you from?" Johnny asked.

"Kentucky. My people are tobacco farm-
ers like most ever'body else there. Me, I

got tired of it. Figured there had to be somethin' better. That's why I joined up."

"How long have you been here?"

"Not long. Little over a week. I'll be glad to be gone. They say the food and conditions is better out at the posts. They don't give us much here, and some of it's so bad nobody can eat it."

Johnny remembered the recruiting sergeant's promise of all he could eat. He wondered how much more of what he had been told was untrue.

Frank picked up the two pairs of trousers and handed one to Johnny. "You'd best learn how to do this. Just do it like I do."

"What do the stripes mean?" Johnny asked, while trying to imitate Frank's folds.

"What stripes? What are you talkin' about?"

"The ones on their sleeves."

"Oh, that. That's rank. Two stripes is a corporal, and three's a sergeant. There's a bunch of other symbols that separate the different kinds of sergeants, but I ain't learned them yet. One thing I do know, the sergeant of this outfit thinks he's just a little under God Almighty Himself."

Johnny laid his pants on top of the pair Frank had finished. "You and him have trouble?"

"Yeah, some. Not over much of nothin', really. We just don't get along."

They finished with the clothes and placed them neatly in the footlocker. Johnny didn't think it could be too much longer before lights-out.

"Is there a privy around, Frank?"

"Yeah. Go out the way you come in and take a left. You'll see it sittin' out there by itself. A lantern'll be hangin' by the door."

∧

SEVERAL MINUTES LATER Johnny returned and saw a cluster of men gathered at the far end of the building, near his bunk. He hurriedly shoved his way through and found Frank holding the end of a pair of trousers while another recruit was trying to pull them away from him. Uniforms were scattered on the floor, and Johnny noticed his footlocker was open.

One of the men grabbed Frank from behind. When Frank turned his head toward him, Johnny saw blood dripping from his nose.

Fury welled up in Johnny, and he leaped, putting his momentum behind his right fist. The blow hit the soldier holding Frank squarely on the temple, and the man crashed to the floor.

Johnny quickly moved around in front of Frank, grabbed the trousers, and yanked mightily. The older recruit who held them came flying, and Johnny hit him in the side. Johnny let go of the pants and was about to hit the man again when a loud whistle blew, accompanied by a shout.

"Atten' ut!"

Everyone standing was like a stone statue—eyes straight ahead, feet together, chest out, and arms to the side—except Johnny. He stood as he was, his fists clenched white, watching a rawboned, gangling soldier with three stripes on his sleeve approach. Two guards with rifles across their arms followed close behind.

Johnny guessed by the way the man swaggered from side to side twirling a black stick that he was the sergeant Frank had spoken of, the one who thought he was just a little under God Himself.

The sergeant stopped in front of the group, tapping the end of the stick against the palm of his left hand. "Animals. Dogs. The scum of the earth. That is what you are. That is what this man's army has been given to make soldiers out of."

His glare found Johnny. "You're new, aren't you?"

Before Johnny could answer, the sergeant pushed one of the recruits to the side and stepped closer. "Why aren't you standing at attention? Are you too stupid to follow a simple order?"

Johnny met the sergeant's eyes evenly. He was still mad, so mad his body trembled. "I don't know anything about any order. These fellows were taking my stuff and..." He almost mentioned Frank's name, then decided against it. If Frank and the sergeant didn't get along, it might be better to leave him out of it. "And I was stopping them. Wouldn't you do the same if somebody was taking your stuff?"

"Silence!" The sergeant's cheeks above his ragged mustache turned red. "You don't question *me* . . . ever! *I* ask the questions around here."

"Permission to speak, sir?"

The voice was Frank's, and Johnny turned to him, as did the sergeant. Blood still dripped from Frank's nose, and his shirt was covered with it.

"What do you have to say, farm boy? I see you've been right in the middle of this little fracas."

Frank remained erect, not even moving his eyes. "Private McBane is tellin' the truth, sir. The men was takin' his things."

A soldier, the same older-looking recruit Johnny had yanked the trousers from and hit in the side, spoke up. "We were just goin' to haze him a bit, Sarge. Give him his initiation into the company like we do all the newcomers. No harm was meant. To-morrow we were gonna give his clothes and beddin' back.

"That one"—he pointed at Johnny—"hit him." He indicated the recruit trying to rise from the floor. "And then he slugged me."

The sergeant's lips curled into a wicked smile. He motioned for the older recruit to stand beside him. "Farm boy...," he said to Frank, then shifted his gaze to Johnny. "McBane? Is that what farm boy said your name was? This man is a veteran of the Civil War and is now enlisting for his third term. He'll be promoted to corporal before he leaves Jefferson Barracks.

"If he says no harm was meant, then that settles it. All new enlistees are hazed in one way or another. When I joined the service, I was no exception. It is obvious to me that you both need a lesson in army discipline."

The sergeant turned to the two soldiers who had followed him in with their guns. "Take them to the bullring. I'll be along shortly."

The Bullring

JOHNNY AND FRANK stood in the center of the sixty-foot-diameter circle known as the bullring. One lantern hung from the ceiling, providing barely enough light to see. The two guards who had escorted them there stood to the side, holding their rifles ready.

A door opened, its rusty hinges making a grating sound, and the sergeant stepped into the building and walked slowly toward the ring. He held a coiled whip in one hand and the black stick in the other.

Johnny burned with anger. Neither he nor Frank had done anything wrong. If anyone needed punishing, it was the recruits who were taking his things, especially the older Civil War veteran the sergeant seemed to think so much of.

Yet what could he do? Two rifles were trained on him. If he broke and ran, maybe they wouldn't really shoot. Perhaps if they did, they would miss. If it was just him, Johnny decided, he'd take the chance. He would leave Jefferson Barracks and the army far behind, never to return. But to run now would put Frank in danger, put him right in the line of fire, and that was a risk Johnny would not take.

The sergeant reached the circle and stepped through the iron fence rails. He carelessly flicked the whip out into a straight line, looked at Frank and Johnny, then popped it.

"This ring is used for training horses, but we've found it works equally well for new recruits of the same intelligence. When I say begin, start running. Each time you hear the crack of my whip, pick up the pace, or feel the tip of my whip on your back.

"Begin!"

Frank started running.

Johnny grudgingly followed in a slow jog, his fury overcoming his fear of the sergeant and making it impossible to show any alacrity.

The whip cracked, and Frank ran faster around the inside of the fence.

Johnny held his pace, rolling his eyes in defiance at the sergeant, who now stood in the center of the ring. He saw the sergeant squint his beady eyes, saw the man raise the whip, and knew he intended to hit him with it. The whip lashed out, and Johnny bolted in an incredible burst of speed.

The pop behind him was loud—and close. Too close.

Johnny resumed his slow jog, warily watching the sergeant. The man scowled and raised the whip again.

A thin smile tightened Johnny's lips. His many fights had taught him that some of the meanest-acting men were the easiest to beat.

Frank had run a lap around the ring ahead of Johnny and passed him. At that moment the sergeant let the whip fly. Johnny dove headlong into the soft dirt, heard the tip of the whip snap above him, then was instantly up, running in the same jog as before, except slower.

The sergeant stomped his foot. "So you want to play games, McBane. I'll teach you to mess with me. Before I'm through, there won't be a thread of hide left on you!"

Time after time the whip popped. Only once did it touch Johnny, and then just his shirt. Sweat beaded the sergeant's brow, and with each swing he cussed.

Frank soon realized that to avoid trouble and not work very hard, he could follow Johnny, staying several yards behind him.

Some time later the sergeant leaned wearily against the fence. Frank and Johnny stood across from him, neither of them very tired.

"Guards," the sergeant shouted. "Tie McBane's wrists to the rail. Tie him tight. Nobody makes a fool out of me. I'll teach him. So help me I'll teach him."

One of the soldiers stepped forward. "You know we can't do that, Sarge. The colonel said there'd be no more lashings without a hearing. If you'd been able to hit him, we'd already be in trouble. Them whip whelps don't go away none too quick.

"Let farm boy go on back to the bar-racks. We'll put McBane in the guardhouse; charge him with insubordination or some-thin'. A week or two in there with nothin' but a little water will take some of that smartness out of him. When we let him out, he'll be lucky if he can walk, let alone run."

The sergeant took his hat off and wiped his forehead with a handkerchief. "All right, then. Take him away. But...," he aimed the black stick at Johnny, "I'm not done with you. Remember that!"

Leaving

^

THREE DAYS LATER the heavy wooden door to Johnny's rock-walled cell opened wide. Sitting in a corner on the dirt floor, Johnny was blinded by the flood of sunlight. He blinked several times, then shielded his eyes with his hands.

A guard he hadn't seen before stepped inside. "Get up. The Seventh Cavalry needs replacements. You've been assigned to Fort Lincoln. Train leaves in four hours."

Johnny slowly got to his feet, unable to fully comprehend what he had been told. In the cell, in the blackness of it, day and

night were one. He didn't know how long
he had been there. Only twice had he been
given water. He had not eaten since the
café in St. Louis where he had foolishly first
thought about joining the military.

Thinking about that and everything else
was all he had been doing. Thinking, and
waiting for a chance to run—to leave the
army—which had to come sooner or later.
And when it did, Johnny intended to undo
the terrible mistake he had made in joining.
He would make it to the St. Louis switchyard, catch another freight somehow, and
go to another town, find a job, maybe even
get back into boxing.

Was this his chance? The guard's rifle
was in a sling across his shoulder. Johnny
knew he could easily knock him down and
be out the door before anyone could stop
him.

A shadow appeared in the doorway, and
it took a moment for Johnny to recognize
Frank's tall, lanky form. "Come on, Johnny.
We're gettin' out of here. They're sendin'
us to the Dakotas to be in Custer's outfit. I
got all your stuff. They're givin' us half our

pay over at the sutler's. We got to hurry."

Custer. Johnny knew the name. Heck, everybody did. The boy general of the Union army, he was called. No one could talk about the Civil War without mentioning George Armstrong Custer and his string of amazing battle victories. After the war, the man's fame continued as a great hunter and frontier Indian fighter.

For a moment Johnny's heart beat rapidly at the thought of traveling west and being in the company of the famous man. But no. He shoved the thought aside. His mind was made up. If what he had been through was any indication of how the army treated its men, he did not want any part of it. The recruiter in St. Louis had lied.

The guard left, and Johnny stepped through the door and stood beside Frank. The sky was clear and the day warm for late February. Most of the snow had melted.

The sun felt good on Johnny's face, and the cool, fresh air was an exhilarating change from the stench of his own excrement and that of others who had been locked inside the rock cell. He felt weak, but not so much that he couldn't carry out his plan to leave.

"Am I free?" Johnny's throat was dry and his voice raspy. "Where's the sergeant? He said he had plenty more in store for me."

Frank handed Johnny one of two canvas bags he carried, then took him by the arm. "Let's go. We got to hurry or they're liable to close the pay window and we won't get none of our money."

Johnny shook loose from his friend. "I don't need the army's money." He looked at the bag in his arms, then let it drop to the ground. "I don't need any uniforms, either. I've had enough. I'm leaving."

"You can't," Frank said. "You don't just quit bein' in the army. Don't you understand? If you leave, you're a deserter. They'll put a reward on your head. When they catch you, they'll send you to prison and put a ball and chain on your leg. I heard they still sometimes brand deserters with a *D* on their hip.

"I know nothin' up to now's been right for you. But that's over with. The sergeant, he's gone. He left a day ago. Had a brother or somebody who was dyin', and he went to see 'im. I finally got permission from the first sergeant to talk to the commander and told him what all happened. He's the one who had you let out. He put you on the same orders as me for Fort Lincoln."

Johnny didn't respond. What Frank said about deserters was probably true, but he had been able to leave Chicago and Julian Dean far behind. There was no reason he could not do the same with the army.

Seeing the stubborn set to Johnny's jaw, Frank continued. "Custer's Seventh Cavalry has the best reputation in the army, and we're goin' to be a part of it. We'll go west and see all there is to see. We may even make history.

"Look here, if you decide to desert, you can do that any old time. Give it a chance and come with me. I told you I heard they treat their men better out at the posts. If we find it ain't so, I may even run with you."

Johnny was quiet. Frank had gone to a lot of trouble to help him. He hesitantly bent over, then picked up his bag. "Maybe you're right. Guess I'll try it—for a while. Right now I need some water, at least a gallon of it. Is there a water bucket or pump close by?"

∧

AT THE SUTLER'S STORE they lined up behind a few others and received their half-month's pay of six dollars and fifty cents. Out of that, each of them had to buy a mandatory uniform-cleaning kit costing two dollars and eighty-five cents.

Tired of being hungry and unsure of when or where his next meal would come from, Johnny spent almost all of the rest of his money on canned peaches, sardines, and beans. He finished eating the contents of one can on the steps outside the store and was about to open another when Frank stopped him.

"What you need is a bath. Can't hardly stand to sit downwind of you. 'Sides, they won't let you on the train unless you're in uniform. Come on. I'll show you where the bathhouse is. If you hurry, we'll make noon mess and you can save the rest of your victuals for the train ride."

Inside the small wooden bathhouse located behind one of the barracks buildings, the air smelled of wood rot and mildew. A square opening in the tin roof provided the inside light.

After taking off his clothes, Johnny pulled one of four evenly spaced ropes hanging from the ceiling. A wooden flume mounted on springs lowered, and a stream of water flowed out. He touched the water with his hand. It was icy.

It took a while for him to build up enough courage to force his body under the frigid spray. A half bar of soap lay on the floor. Johnny picked it up and washed himself as thoroughly and as quickly as he could.

Finished bathing, he dug through his bag with chattering teeth trying to find a blanket or towel to dry himself with. There was none, so he hurriedly put on his uniform and stepped outside into the sun to pull on his socks and boots.

Frank grinned, watching his friend's shaking hands. "Water's a mite cold, ain't it? But you sure look and smell better, 'cept your skin's a little blue."

Johnny eyed his friend coolly. "I'm glad you're enjoying yourself." He finished tying his bootlaces and stood up. The pants were baggy and the boots two sizes too big, but the gray flannel shirt fit about right. He reached in the bag and took out a wool coat and cap and put them on. "How do I look?"

"Plumb purty, 'cept you need your belt on. If they's any girls where we're goin', you'll have to beat 'em off with a stick. The ladies like men in uniform, you know. I heard tell it does somethin' to 'em."

"Well." Johnny blushed. "A girl is the last thing I need. I'm starving. Where's the mess hall?"

Johnny's first army meal was cold corn and bread sopped with gravy made from nothing but hot water and flour, but it was filling, and he ate until he could hold no more.

An hour later, he and Frank were settled into a wagon for the ride to the train depot. Johnny felt good. He was full, clean, and, best of all, he was leaving Jefferson Barracks. And then there was Frank. Although he'd only known Frank a short time, he liked him, and it was good to have someone to talk to.

The wagon creaked along slowly, and Johnny's thoughts wandered. *Custer, the Dakotas, Fort Lincoln.* What would life be like there?

Fort Abraham Lincoln

^

THE LOCOMOTIVE whistle blew as the train's steel wheels slid to a stop on the icy rails. Johnny wiped at the fog on the window, trying to look out. All he could see was a blurred white landscape.

Frank stood up and took his duffel bag in his arms. "We're here, Johnny. This's got to be Bismarck. Fort Lincoln should be just across the river. Least that's what the conductor told me."

Johnny rose, picking up his own bag. He hoped Frank was right. The three-day train trip had not been pleasant. There were more passengers than seats, and they had spent the majority of the trip either standing or sitting in the aisle. Neither of them had been able to get much sleep, and food had only been doled out at a couple of the water stops.

Frank waited for an opening in the aisle traffic, then he and Johnny edged into the line of off-loading passengers. They stepped off the train into soft, deep snow.

A building made of logs faced them, and a man with a long red beard and wearing a large buffalo coat stepped off the veranda and walked toward them. He removed his right mitten and held out his hand, smiling.

"Name's Riley, Josh Riley, but ever'body calls me Crazy Jim 'cause I like to eat rattlesnakes. Who you be?"

Frank shook hands and introduced himself, then Johnny. Crazy Jim put his mitten back on. "I'm here from the fort. They sent me to see if they was any new recruits. Looks like you two young pups is it. Am I right?"

"As far as we know, sir," Frank answered.

"Don't you be callin' me sir. I'm a no-body, just like you. I used to be a corporal, till I got drunk and told an officer what I thought of him. Now I'm just a nobody like you."

Large flakes of snow started to fall, and Crazy Jim looked at the sky. "Gonna be a cold one tonight. Liable to be a blizzard. You two come along with me, and I'll he'p get you settled in."

"Is Custer at the fort?" Johnny asked. "I mean, is he really there now?"

"Naw, Custer's in New York or Washington or somewheres. Major Reno's in command of the Seventh till he gets back. 'Fore you start gettin' all excited about Custer, you'd just as well know that a lot of the men don't like him. He's plumb full of himself and hard on men and horses, too. Why, I seen him make a soldier wear a vinegar barrel for a week, just for gettin' a little drunk. Wasn't nothin' but his feet and head showin'."

"But he's famous," Johnny exclaimed. "He won every battle he fought in the war, didn't he?"

Crazy Jim snorted. "Custer's no coward, to be sure, but that don't make him no saint, either. Men that know him better'n me say he ain't nothin' but a glory hound, takin' credit where it ain't due. They say he couldn't care less what happens to the men under him. You think what you want, but if'n I was you, I'd keep it to myself."

The three crossed the railroad tracks and were soon walking on the thick ice of the Missouri River. A small rowboat carried them across the narrow, unfrozen channel in the middle, and after they hiked a short distance down the far side, Fort Lincoln appeared.

The fort was on a broad plain located between the river and a gentle slope heading to tableland on the west. It wasn't at all what Johnny expected. There were no high walls, no gates, and no guards. Instead, several buildings were loosely arranged around a large piece of open ground in the center.

Seven frame houses edged the open ground on the west. On the east side were three large barracks similar to the ones at Jefferson, only bigger. Behind them, near the river, sprawled stables and corrals full of horses. To the south were a few more buildings, but Johnny had no idea what they were. Except for the open ground in the center, the place looked more like a small town than an army post.

Crazy Jim stopped not far from the first barracks and pointed at a lone square structure near the road. "See that buildin' over yonder with that there flagpole in front of it? That be the post headquarters. Supper'll be on soon, and you two is gonna need your butter allowance money or you won't get no butter.

"Now the both of ya get on over there and ask the first sergeant for it, then come on back here to the barracks. I'll be waitin' fer ya."

Frank started toward the headquarters building. Johnny took a few steps, then turned back to Crazy Jim. "Are you sure we need to see him now? We can get along without butter for a few days. We don't want to be a bother to anyone."

"A' course I'm sure. I won't have it no other way. Ever'body else gets their money and so should you. Now you go on over there and ask him for it. I'll be waitin' fer ya."

Johnny walked slowly toward the building. His experience with the sergeant at Jefferson Barracks had taught him to stay as far away from sergeants as he could.

Frank stepped up on the plank porch in front of the headquarters building and waited for Johnny to join him. Then he knocked on the door.

"Come in." The voice was loud, raspy, and impatient sounding.

Johnny and Frank entered and closed the door behind them. A short, bald, squinty-eyed man wearing thick glasses sat behind a wooden desk looking at some papers. He spoke without looking up. "What do you want?"

Frank stood at attention, clicking his heels together. "Sir, we just made it here off the train, and we've come for our butter money. Crazy—uh, I mean Josh Riley said we should see the first sergeant about it."

The man looked up and removed his glasses, a grin on his face. "So Crazy Jim sent you, did he? And I guess you two really think you are goin' to receive the money for your butter?"

"Yes, sir." Frank stood even straighter than before.

Johnny was not sure what to think, but nothing about this felt right. He took a step to bring himself even with Frank. "We're sorry to have bothered you, sir. We don't need any money. Please excuse us." Johnny headed for the door.

"Just a minute, lad."

Johnny stopped.

"I'm the first sergeant, and ol' Jim needs a lesson, to be sure." The man reached in his pocket, took out two silver dollars, and laid them on the desk. "There now, this time the joke's on him. You lads take your butter money and be sure to show it to him."

Frank and Johnny stood still.

"Go on now, take it. I be givin' you an order to take it."

Frank sheepishly picked up the coins, realizing he and Johnny had been had.

"Thank you, sir. We'll show the money to him."

Outside, the two walked slowly toward the first barracks. A group of soldiers was waiting there by the steps, some of them pointing and laughing. As they drew closer, Crazy Jim led the others in a chant, standing in front of them like a chorus conductor.

"The butter boys are comin', yes-sir-ree. Green behind the ears for all of us to see."

Johnny set his bag down. It looked like Frank was wrong about things being better out here than they had been at Jefferson Barracks. He braced himself for the trouble he felt was bound to come.

The soldiers finally grew quiet, and Crazy Jim looked at the two. "Did ya get yer butter money like I told ya to do?"

A few men chuckled, until Frank and Johnny held out their hands, revealing the coins. Johnny cleared his throat and managed a smile. "The first sergeant said to be sure and show you the money he gave us. A dollar apiece should buy a lot of butter and still leave some left over. Thanks for sending us to him."

The soldiers roared with laughter, some of them doubled over with it, holding their sides. Crazy Jim's face turned as red as his mustache, and in a few moments he left, walking hastily toward the headquarters building.

A lean soldier with rusty brown hair stepped up and shook hands with Frank and Johnny. "I'm Corporal Kelley, and that's the most fun we've had in a month. Don't worry about Crazy Jim; he'll come around. You boys go on inside by the fire. I'm goin' to find out what company you're in. If I can I'll keep you here in L Company with me. Not every day a couple of newcomers get the best of Crazy Jim."

Kelley hurried off, and Johnny and Frank walked up the steps of the barracks, followed by the rest of the men. Inside, the bunks were arranged much like they had been at Jefferson Barracks, except the atmosphere was homier.

Each soldier's bunk area was personalized, some having a picture or two tacked to the wall or a few books stacked on a shelf above the beds. A fire blazed in the potbellied stove in the center of the room, and everyone gathered around it, pulling off their coats.

Corporal Kelley returned shortly, informing Frank and Johnny that they would be staying in L Company. He assigned them bunks in a cool corner. All of the bunks near the stove were already taken.

Johnny was relieved there were no more incidents. Unlike the men at Jefferson Barracks, these soldiers seemed friendly enough. Soon Johnny and Frank followed the others to the company mess hall located behind the barracks, and after eating a meal of corn bread and slumgullion stew, the entire garrison assembled outside for sunset retreat and roll call. Johnny marveled at the number of men gathered, guessing there to be two hundred or more.

Having no idea what he was doing, Johnny tried to imitate Frank's and the other men's reactions to the various commands being yelled out by the soldier standing in front of them. When they stood up

straight—or relaxed with their hands behind their backs—so did Johnny. And when
his name was called, he shouted, "Here,"
like the others before him had done.

Roll call finally finished, and the forma-
tion was dismissed. Johnny and Frank followed the company into the barracks. They
went to their bunks and had just started to
unpack their bags when Corporal Kelley
and another soldier walked up.

"Boys," Kelley said. "This is Sergeant
O'Connell. He runs L Company."

Frank moved to the end of his bunk.
"I'm Private Gann, sir."

Sergeant O'Connell shook Frank's hand,
then faced Johnny. He was a slender man
of medium height, with a long face, black-
browed gray eyes, and deep creases cut into
the corners of his mouth.

Johnny nodded, still unsure about sergeants. "I'm Johnny McBane."

"No," the sergeant reprimanded. "You
are *Private* McBane." He turned to Kelley.
"Have them both report to the post
surgeon in the morning for their phys-
icals."

"I already had one of those, sir," Johnny said, not wanting to go through it again.

"I'm sure you have, but not here, and here I'm responsible for the fitness of my men."

Sergeant O'Connell studied Johnny a long moment. "How old are you?"

Johnny thought back to his conversation with the recruiter in St. Louis and for the first time realized how easy it would be to get out of the army if he chose to. The recruiter had wanted him to be twenty-one, so that must be the age he needed to be to join. All he had to do was tell the sergeant his real age, at least as close as he knew it, and he was free.

But the supper had been good, and so far no one here at Fort Lincoln had mistreated him. Crazy Jim's joke had backfired, and even if it hadn't, the consequences might not have been as severe as Johnny had at first believed. No, he had already made the decision to give the army another try, and for the time being, he would stick to it.

"I'm twenty-one."

"You wouldn't lie to me, would you?" O'Connell's voice was sharp, with a faint note of rancor. "I have ways of checking. You know you can join at eighteen with written consent from your parents?"

"I don't have any folks, sir."

"You don't, huh? I'll see about that." He shifted his eyes to include Frank in his next statement. "You will find I'm easy to get along with as long as you do what you are told.

"In a couple of months the entire Seventh Cavalry will ride against the Sioux. I need men who follow orders, men who know what they are doing and can fight. If I were you, I would use this time to learn everything I could about being a soldier. If you're lucky, it might be enough to save your life."

Sergeant O'Connell left the building. Corporal Kelley waited until the sound of his steps died. "The sarge isn't that bad. I've been around worse. He'll loosen up a little once he gets to know you. Don't cross him, though. He's one heck of a fighter. One of the main reasons they made him sergeant was because he could handle the hard cases that come in."

Crazy Jim came into the barracks, stopped by the stove, and took off his snow-covered mittens and hat. His voice was loud. "Heard they's now near fifteen thousand miners in the Black Hills a-lookin' fer gold. Reckon ol' Sittin' Bull won't stand fer it. We may be goin' after him sooner'n we think. It's too dad-blamed cold to go to chasin' injuns. My old bones can't take it like they used to."

Johnny laid a pair of trousers on the bed. He wanted to ask Crazy Jim about the Black Hills, about the Sioux and Sitting Bull, but he thought the man might still be mad about the butter money. Corporal Kelley left to go to his bunk. Johnny hesitantly followed him as far as the stove, where Jim was shoving a stick in the fire.

"Jim, would you tell me about Sitting Bull? I've heard of him but don't know anything about him. Sergeant O'Connell said we were going after the Sioux in a couple of months. Is Sitting Bull a chief or something?"

Crazy Jim's stern expression relaxed into a smile. He looked past Johnny, down the aisle at Frank.

"You just as well get on over here, too. It's Sittin' Bull, Crazy Horse, and Gall who're gonna scalp ya, cut your eyes out, and open up your belly for the crows. You might as well know somethin' about 'em."

Frank joined Johnny, and they sat down on the end of a bunk while Crazy Jim took off his coat and pulled up a chair. Most of the soldiers who were lounging on their beds turned their attention to him.

"Ya know about the Fetterman Massacre down by Fort Phil Kearny in '66, don't ya?"

Johnny and Frank shook their heads.

"Well, to give you an idea what them Sioux can do, I'll tell ya. Cap'n Fetterman and about eighty men was sent out to rescue a wood-cuttin' party. Crazy Horse and a few other Oglalas tricked him into chasin' 'em. The cap'n shoulda know'd better, but he didn't. A bunch more injuns was waitin' fer the soldiers to come through so they could ambush 'em.

"And that's what they done. They killed

ever' last one of Fetterman's bunch, includin' Fetterman hisself. Then them injuns stripped 'em naked, gutted 'em, and crushed their skulls. They tore them soldiers' bodies to pieces, cuttin' off their legs and hands and ears and noses. They even cut their teeth out and put their brains on the rocks."

Crazy Jim stopped for a second, noting Frank's and Johnny's wide eyes. "I tell ya, I ain't lyin'. And them Sioux is still out there. They're right out there in the dark right now, just waitin' fer ya like they do."

Johnny swallowed hard. He wasn't sure whether to believe Jim or not, but the story could be true. "Was Sitting Bull there?"

"Naw." Crazy Jim shifted his weight and his chair squeaked. "That was some a' Red Cloud's bunch. Sittin' Bull and Gall and Crazy Horse are worse'n him. They'll set ya on fire while you're still alive. They'll put burnin' coals in your mouth, and they'll—"

"That's enough, Jim," Corporal Kelley half shouted from his bunk.

"Well, it's true, ain't it? You tell 'em if I done told 'em a single lie."

"It's true enough, but it's not just those two going after the Sioux. We are all going, and we don't want to hear any more about it. We're going to fight the Indians, whip them, and make sure they stay on the reservation where they belong."

"Where is the Sioux reservation?" Frank asked.

Crazy Jim rose from his chair, opened the stove door, and spit a stream of tobacco juice into the fire. "It's the Black Hills country and on east to the Missouri and north to the Grand River."

"But...didn't you say fifteen thousand miners were in the Black Hills?" Johnny asked, confused.

"That's what I done said."

"But if that's Sioux land, what are the miners doing there?"

"Lookin' fer gold, mostly, I reckon. The government tried to buy them hills and the Sioux wouldn't sell, so the miners go there anyway and the government kinda looks the other way. 'Cept ol' Sittin' Bull and his bunch don't look the other way. They're mad about most ever'thin'. The railroad, the Black Hills, and the whites bein' in their old huntin' grounds on the buffalo plains east a' the Bighorns.

"Reckon Kelley's right, though," Crazy Jim continued. "This summer we'll round up all them renegade devils, and what we ain't killed, we'll put back on the reservation. Oughtn't be too much trouble if we can catch 'em. Injuns would rather run than fight.

"I hear they're gonna bring in all twelve companies of the Seventh fer the first time and get shed a' the Sioux once and fer all. Won't *that* be a party now. Ol' Sittin' Bull won't never know what hit him."

The room was still. What Johnny had learned, if it was true, did not seem right. The government didn't want the Indians on its land, so why did it allow whites to trespass on Sioux land?

Johnny started to state his thoughts, then changed his mind. He really didn't know enough about it to argue, and his views might turn the men against him.

Some of them likely had friends or relatives who had been killed by Indians, and all the talk in the world would not change their minds about them.

He stood. "I guess I better get my clothes folded and put up."

Crazy Jim looked up from the tobacco sack he had his fingers in. "Yeah, reckon you'd better get it done 'fore lights-out. Guess you and Frank'll get your brandin' in the mornin'."

"Brandin'?" Frank frowned. "What brandin'?"

"Well, ever'thin' that belongs to the government's got a U.S. brand on it. Saddles, blankets, horses, ever'thin'. Why, ever'one of us here done been marked. It's just somethin' the army does. Iron's red hot and smokin', and when the doc puts it on your skin the burnin' flesh stinks somethin' terrible. It don't hurt fer too long, though, so long as you put a little axle grease on it."

Johnny could not stop a smile from spreading across his face. Frank had told him about deserters sometimes being branded, but *this* had to be another one of Crazy Jim's jokes.

"You don't believe me, do ya? You think I'm tryin' to trick ya like I done with yer butter money."

Crazy Jim rose from his chair and started unbuckling his belt. "Well, I'll show ya what you're gonna get. You ain't gonna be grinnin' when the doc sets that iron on you in the mornin'. You're gonna be yellin', that's what you're gonna be doin'."

It took a while because after Crazy Jim had dropped his pants, he had to take his shirt off and pull down his long underwear. Finally, he exposed his hairy right hip.

Frank and Johnny started laughing, and everyone in the barracks quickly gathered around for a look. The red ink Jim had obviously used to make the brand was smeared, and there was a run below each of the two letters.

"What?" Crazy Jim shouted angrily, trying his best to twist his head around his middle so he could see his behind. "It's there, I tell ya. Might be a little rough. The doc, ya know, why, he was drunk when he burned me. He done a real sloppy job."

Every soldier in the room was laughing. Johnny laughed so hard tears came to his eyes.

Eventually Jim pulled up his underwear. "It ain't none a' my fault. The doc done it, I tell ya, and the same thing's gonna happen to you in the mornin'. It is. I swear it!"

Horses

^

JOHNNY WATCHED as Frank put his left foot in the stirrup of the McClellan army saddle. The young sorrel cavalry horse he was trying to mount shied sideways, and Frank had to hop on his right foot to keep from falling.

Crazy Jim and a few other soldiers gathered around the small circular corral snickered. Corporal Kelley, who sat on top of the fence, yelled at Frank. "Pull his head into you with the reins, grab his mane, and swing on."

Frank did as he was told. His backside had no more than hit the saddle seat when the sorrel put his nose to the ground and bucked in a high jump, bringing all four of his feet off the ground.

The horse came down front feet first with his rear high in the air, and Frank flew over the horse's head like a boulder pushed off a ledge, landing face first in the deep black mud. The soldiers howled with glee, and Johnny could not help but grin as Frank crawled to his knees, wiping at the mud on his face with the clumps of mud in his hands.

"That's all right," Frank told Johnny. "You just remember who's next."

Johnny's smile vanished. He knew he didn't have a chance. If Frank, who had ridden lots of horses on his folks' farm in Kentucky, could be thrown so easily, there was no way Johnny, who had never been on a horse, was going to be able to stay in the saddle. He doubted if he would even be able to get seated in it.

"OK, McBane," Corporal Kelley said,

obviously enjoying the entertainment. "The horse is gettin' old waitin' on you."

Johnny looked at him. "Shouldn't I learn how to ride on something gentler? Maybe you've got a horse somewhere around here that's real old and slow."

"Cav'ry don't need no old, slow hosses to chase injuns on," Crazy Jim shouted. "Why, my grandma could ride that little ol' pony, and she's purt' near ninety-two."

The soldiers, including Kelley, laughed, and Johnny could see there was no way of getting out of it. These fellows had to have their fun, and for this Sunday afternoon, the only free time any of them'd had in days, he and Frank were it.

Johnny found he couldn't really blame them. He had been at Fort Lincoln only a little more than a week, and already the daily routine had become dull and monotonous. Every day was like the day before.

Each morning at six the trumpeters sounded reveille. After roll call, mess was at six-thirty. At seven-thirty came fatigue call, and Johnny and Frank were always assigned to the kitchen detail to chop wood for the cookstoves, carry water, peel potatoes, and wash dishes.

Eight o'clock was sick call; nine was the assembly of the guard. Nine-forty-five was recall from fatigue detail, and at ten was drill. At eleven-thirty was recall from drill, and eleven-forty-five, first sergeant's call. Noon mess was at one o'clock, and at two it was back to fatigue duty in the kitchen, except for Fridays and Saturdays, when everyone cleaned the barracks and other post facilities for Sunday morning's nine o'clock inspection.

Four-fifteen was recall from afternoon fatigue, and four-thirty was stable call, when all the soldiers went to the corrals to groom and care for the horses. Evening mess was at five-fifteen, and assembly of the entire garrison occurred at five minutes before sundown. Sunset was retreat and roll call; nine o'clock, last roll call; and nine-thirty, lights-out.

For the first couple of days the schedule was confusing, but Frank and Johnny quickly learned to listen for the sound of the trumpets and do what the other soldiers did when they heard them. Now, in the short time they had been there, the schedule had become so ingrained they did not have to think about it.

Frank got out of the corral, and Johnny climbed into it, stepping cautiously toward the sorrel. He reached for the ends of the reins, which were on the ground, and the horse snorted, then whirled and ran, splattering him with mud from his hooves.

Johnny spent some time trying to catch the horse, without any success. Finally, Crazy Jim opened the gate and walked in, a coiled rope in his hand. He approached the horse and twirled the lasso lazily above his head as he talked.

"It's a mighty embarrassin' day when a soldier in the Seventh Cav' can't even catch a horse, let alone ride him."

The loop shot from his hand and settled evenly around the horse's neck. "Reckon I'll have to play nursemaid for the greenhorns this here army keeps takin' in. Embarrassin', that's what it is. Plumb embarrassin'."

Crazy Jim pulled the rope tight and

walked toward the horse. He grabbed the reins, slid the loop off the horse's head, and looked behind at Johnny. "Well, climb on. We ain't got all day to fool with ya."

Johnny advanced to the side of the horse, his heart beating rapidly. He started to put his foot in the stirrup when Jim hollered, "You don't know nothin', do ya? You're done on the wrong side. You get on a horse on the left. How you gonna chase injuns if ya can't even figure out what side you got to get on your horse?"

The horse pawed the ground with his right front foot, and Johnny took a step back and glared across the saddle seat at Jim. He was beginning to get irritated, yet he knew what Jim said was true. He hardly knew one end of a horse from the other, and his being in the cavalry was ridiculous.

Fighting down his emotions, Johnny moved to the other side, put his foot in the stirrup, grabbed the horse's mane like Frank had done, and swung into the saddle. Crazy Jim let loose the bridle and hightailed it out of the corral. The reins Johnny had not remembered to grab dropped to the ground.

Then everything was a blur.

The sorrel reared on his hind legs and tottered back and forth while Johnny leaned as far forward as he could and wrapped his arms tightly around the horse's neck. For a moment it seemed the horse was sure to fall over backward and crush him—then at last he came down hard on his front feet and bucked in a high, twisting jump.

The horse was too powerful, and the move too sudden. Johnny's grip was broken, and he was thrown into the air. He landed on his back, felt the wind explode from his lungs, and looked up to see one of the horse's hooves coming straight down for the middle of his face.

Johnny closed his eyes, rolled to the side, and wrapped his arm over his head. The hoof struck him just below the shoulder with a sickening thud, and pain shot through his body. He gasped and rolled again, hoping to avoid being stomped some more.

The horse trotted off, and in a few

moments Johnny sat up, clutching his arm with his left hand and trying to regain the air that had been knocked from him.

Frank, Corporal Kelley, and Crazy Jim raced into the corral. Frank kneeled beside Johnny. "You all right? Looked like he stepped right on your head."

Johnny tried to manage a smile against the pain. "It probably would hurt less if he had."

A loud shout came from behind them. "What in the devil's going on here?" Sergeant O'Connell stepped through the corral gate. He looked down at Johnny and then across at the sorrel standing quietly against the far fence.

Frank helped Johnny to his feet.

"I'm waiting, Kelley," Sergeant O'Connell scolded. "You better have an explanation for this. You know good and well I gave orders that no one ride that sorrel. That horse has already put two soldiers in the hospital and crippled a third. Nobody's ever stayed on him more than a few seconds."

Kelley stared at the ground like a small

child in big trouble. Crazy Jim started to inch away nonchalantly.

"Stay right here, Private Riley. Don't you take another step. You were also aware of my orders."

Crazy Jim stopped. Sweat beaded his forehead although the day was cool. Kelley was nervously rubbing his hands together. It was obvious the matter was serious.

"Well?" O'Connell asked, looking again at Kelley.

"Uh, uh, we—we ..."

"It's my fault, sir," Johnny blurted out. "I'd heard about the horse and thought I could ride him. No one's to blame but me. I didn't know about the orders."

Sergeant O'Connell stared at Johnny. "You're lying and you know it, just like you lied to me about your age.

"Look, these men are veteran soldiers. There is no reason for you to protect them. Orders are orders and they know the consequences of disobedience. Now tell me the truth. What happened here? Who told you and Gann to ride that horse?"

Johnny's gaze was steady and fearless. "Like I said, sir, no one's to blame but me."

Sergeant O'Connell poked Johnny in the chest with his finger. "I hate liars. One of these days you and I are going to butt heads, and you are going to learn what some others here at Fort Lincoln have had to learn the hard way."

The evening mess bell rang, and the sergeant turned to Kelley and Jim. "If I ever see anything like this again, I'll have you both court-martialed. Now get that horse put up and see that McBane gets to the hospital. The way he's holding that arm, it may be broken."

Corporal Kelley and Crazy Jim moved fast, both of them going for the horse to put as much distance as possible between them and the sergeant. O'Connell left the corral, and Johnny and Frank walked to where the other soldiers had been gathered near the gate. They were gone.

Johnny leaned against a post. His arm throbbed, but he didn't think it was broken.

"Heck of a chance you took," Frank said. "That sergeant don't seem like nobody to fool with. You're lucky you got by with it like you did."

"Yeah, I guess. But it didn't seem right for Kelley and Jim to get into too much trouble. They were only having fun."

"Their fun was paid out of our pocket. It's a wonder that horse didn't kill us both." Frank scraped the bottom of his boot on a fence rail to remove some of the mud. He grinned. "You know, I did ride him longer than you. You didn't make it through the first jump and I stayed on till he hit the ground."

"Yeah, but at least you had the reins."

They opened and closed the gate and were halfway to the barracks when Kelley and Crazy Jim caught up with them.

Jim slapped Johnny on the back. "That there was the finest thing I ever see'd a body do. You just standin' there in front of the sergeant, cool as the dawn frost. Why, he'd had me in the guardhouse in a hurry, I'm tellin' ya, and Kelley here'd lost his stripes by mornin'."

He grabbed Frank's shoulder. "You, too, Gann. You coulda spoke up, but you didn't.

You boys is all right. Ain't never seen none no better."

Kelley moved in front of Johnny to face him. "Thanks. I owe you. Jim's right. I was in mighty big trouble. I shouldn't have put you boys on that horse. Guess we all just wanted a laugh. I didn't figure O'Connell would show up."

Johnny touched his shoulder. "Maybe sometime you'll get a gentle horse and teach me how to ride?"

"It's a promise. You can count on it."

Johnny stepped around him and started toward the barracks.

"Hey, wait a minute," Kelley called. "I got orders to take you to the hospital, and like you already know, I always follow orders."

Fatigue Duty

^

JOHNNY WORKED steadily, chopping up the large clods of earth with a hoe. But his mind wasn't on his task. He was thinking about the life he had left behind in Chicago.

He didn't miss it. Didn't miss the crowds, the drunks, the gamblers, prostitutes, and thieves. It seemed everyone there was hustling for a dollar, and to most of them, it didn't make any difference how they got it.

Johnny knew he had been no different. It took money to survive, and that, along with the desire to be somebody important, had been the motivation for just about everything he did. Here at Fort Lincoln he felt none of that. His basic physical needs were met, and he didn't have a lot of use for the money he had. Instead of pushing to get ahead of anyone else, he was comfortable as part of a company of men whose daily lives differed little from his own.

"Johnny," Frank said, pressing a shovel deep into the black soil with his foot. He stepped back from it, took his handkerchief from his pocket, and wiped his brow. "This here work makes me feel like I'm back on the farm in Kentucky. I spent dang near my whole life shovelin' or hoein'. Then I join the army to get away from it, and look what the sergeant's done got me doin'."

"It's because you're so good at it." Johnny grinned, turning over a half-frozen clump of grassy soil. "Just think about all the fresh vegetables you're going to eat out of this garden when summer finally gets here."

"I guess you're forgettin' we ain't gonna

be here at the fort come summer. We're gonna be out chasin' Indians."

"Yeah, I forgot about that. But maybe we won't be gone too long." Johnny stepped closer to his friend. "Does that stuff Crazy Jim said about the miners being on the Sioux reservation bother you?"

"Not near as much as what he said happened to Captain Fetterman and his men. I'm still havin' nightmares about that. A few nights ago I had one so bad it woke me up. You were there with me, and there were Indians everywhere. Hundreds of them, thousands. They were screamin' and yellin'.

"Our horses were lyin' dead in front of us, shot full of arrows. We were fightin', shootin' as fast as we could, and then... well... well, it don't matter."

"What happened, Frank?"

"Aw, nothin'. It was only a dream. Forget it."

"Tell me."

"Well, you... you went down, Johnny. You..."

Frank grabbed the shovel and turned, ramming the ground and tilling the soil as if the earth had become an enemy. Johnny stood watching. It bothered him to see Frank so upset over a dream, but he couldn't think of anything to say that would help.

They had finished turning over the sod on about half of the garden plot in silence when Frank stopped work again. He sat down on the ground. "What are you gonna do when your hitch in the army is over?"

Johnny leaned against the hoe. "I don't know. Haven't thought about it much. I kind of like it here. Maybe I'll sign up again."

"Yeah, me, too. Except Corporal Kelley came to me with an idea that don't sound too bad. He's from Texas, you know, and he's due to get out of the army about the same time we are. He says there's land down there in Texas just for the takin'. Miles and miles of it.

"He thinks we—and he talked about you and Crazy Jim, too—ought to go down there and start a big ranch. If we went to savin' our money now, he says we'll have enough to stock the ranch plumb full of cattle and horses. We can hire some hands to do the work, and all we'll have to do is sit around in the sunshine countin' our money whenever we want to sell off a year-lin' or two."

Johnny smiled. "You know how much I know about cattle and horses."

"Doesn't matter, Johnny. I'm a farmer. I don't know nothin' about a big ranch. You and me can learn together."

Shooting

^

THE MID-APRIL morning was cool, and Johnny turned up the collar on the heavy buffalo coat he had been issued. He was beginning to wonder if spring ever came to Dakota Territory or if the wind ever stopped blowing. Chicago had been cold, but not like this.

"All right," Corporal Kelley said, and handed Frank and Johnny each a cartridge. "You both have a brand-new Springfield carbine and a Colt revolver, and this is probably the only practice you're going to get with them unless you buy your own ammunition. Forty-fives are expensive, and the army don't believe in wasting them."

Kelley moved behind them. "Each of you gets to shoot ten shots, five with your carbine and five with your 'thumb-buster.' Go ahead and load up your long gun, but don't fire until I say so."

Johnny looked at the copper cartridge in his mitten. Until now, he had never held a gun in his life and had no idea how to load one. He watched as Frank pulled the hammer back on his carbine, lifted the breechblock, and pushed the bullet into the barrel. Johnny removed his mittens and did the same with his rifle, except at first he tried to put the shell in backward and had to turn it around to get it to fit.

He closed the breechblock like Frank had done and brought the butt of the gun against his shoulder while placing his index finger through the trigger guard.

The rifle leaped in his hands, making a thunderous roar. Frank dropped to the ground, and Johnny stood there looking at the smoking muzzle, unable to believe the gun had gone off.

Corporal Kelley ran to Frank and rolled him over. "Where you hit? I don't see any blood. Talk to me! Tell me where..."

Frank rose to a sitting position. "I'm not hit, just tryin' to keep it that way." He grabbed his rifle out of the snow, wiped it off, and got to his feet. Johnny had not moved. His eyes were wide and blank, and the color in his face was gone.

Kelley marched over to him. "You weren't supposed to shoot until I said to. How come you shot?"

Johnny didn't answer, didn't seem to even hear the question. Kelley jerked the carbine out of his hands. "Are you listenin' to me? I want to know why you shot."

"I...I don't know. I didn't mean to pull the trigger. It...it just went off."

Kelley shook his head. After a long moment of hesitation he handed the rifle back. "See to it that you don't let her go off again. You could have killed me or Gann or yourself. You're gonna have to be more careful."

Johnny nodded. Corporal Kelley waved at Frank. "Your turn. Get ready."

Frank grinned. "Not unless you promise you won't let Johnny have another shell till I'm done and back in the barracks."

Kelley scratched his cheek. "Umm, might be a good idea. You shoot all your rounds first, then you and me will get on back to the fort and hide behind something while he shoots his." The corporal kept his face straight. "May be best if we tell everybody in Bismarck they ought to hide, too."

"You're both real funny," Johnny said. "It's just that I've never shot a gun before. I don't know what I'm doing."

"All the more reason for us to hightail it outta here while you're practicin'," Frank said, raising his rifle. He took aim at a small wooden crate in the distance. "Don't take your eyes off him, Kelley. I can't shoot good when I'm worried."

"I won't. Bullet or no bullet, it's plain to see he's plumb dangerous.

"You ready?"

"Yep. Whole lot bigger target than them squirrels' heads I used to shoot at in Kentucky."

"Fire."

Frank's gun boomed, and a piece of wood flew off the crate. He fired four more rounds, hitting the box each time, then switched to his revolver. He wasn't as good with it and only managed two hits out of five.

Corporal Kelley approached Johnny, who stood a few yards behind them. He started to offer him a cartridge, then pulled his hand back and turned his head to look at Frank. "I don't know. Maybe we better notify everybody before he loads up."

Frank handed Kelley his two guns. "You hold these and give me his shells. I've been thinkin' about it and decided the safest place to be is right here beside him."

His eyes met Johnny's. "I'll help you, if you want. I'm not much with a pistol, as you seen, but maybe Kelley would help you with that."

Johnny's rigid expression relaxed. Sometimes he forgot that these two really were his friends. Kelley handed him a bullet. "Carbine first, then your Colt. Now you're gonna have to pay attention and remember what we tell you."

"I will," Johnny said, pulling back the hammer on the Springfield. He turned a step as he raised the breechblock, pointing the muzzle at Kelley's middle.

Frank grabbed the barrel and forced it down. "First thing is, you never point a gun at anything you don't figure to shoot."

"But I wasn't ready. I haven't even got it loaded yet."

"Don't matter. Nobody wants a gun pointin' at 'em, loaded or not."

Johnny kept the muzzle down and finished loading. He paid close attention as Frank showed him how to let the hammer down easy so the gun would not fire. Then Frank explained how to use the sights.

Finally ready, Johnny fired, then loaded and shot again. He had fired his last carbine round when Crazy Jim showed up.

"I been watchin' from back there a ways, and you ain't hit close to nothin'. What you gonna do when ol' Sittin' Bull and a couple hunnerd a' his braves come ridin' down to lift yer hair? You'd be 'bout as well off to throw rocks at 'em."

Johnny looked away. Crazy Jim was always full of stories and mischief, but today the hard truth of his words struck deep. What *was* he going to do?

He realized he hadn't found a single thing about soldiering he was really good at. And he had no desire to fight or kill any Indians. Yet he didn't want to leave the army. The last few weeks had given him a sense of belonging he had never known before. L Company was like the family he'd never had, and Fort Lincoln was his home. He had friends, a good bed, plenty to eat, and a daily routine that was so structured it left little time to think about anything else.

Crazy Jim reached in his coat pocket and took out a cartridge. "Here ya go," he said, tossing it to Johnny. "This here's on me. When you're dead and yer body is all cut up in tiny pieces, can't nobody say Josh Riley didn't try to help you all he could by givin' ya some ammunition to practice with. You just go ahead and shoot it."

With some difficulty Johnny managed to pry out the swollen copper hull in his carbine and reload it. He took a few steps toward the crate target, cocked the gun, and aimed carefully.

He pulled the trigger. Sparks from the breechblock flew into his face, and the gun's horrendous report deafened him, seeming to shake his brain around inside his head as if it were a marble in a bucket. His shoulder and his bruised arm, which he thought had healed after being stepped on by the sorrel horse, tingled numbly from the recoil, and he barely managed to keep from dropping the carbine.

He looked around. Corporal Kelley and Crazy Jim were laughing hysterically. Jim had his hat off and was joyfully stomping the ground.

It took a few seconds before it struck Johnny what had happened. The cartridge had been much more powerful than the others he had shot. It was just another one of Crazy Jim's tricks. The man had known what was going to happen when he gave Johnny the cartridge.

Johnny tramped toward Jim, his ears still ringing loudly. "You could have killed me! It's a miracle the gun didn't blow up in my face. I should..."

Crazy Jim held up his hands and backed away. "How was I supposed to know that there bullet was so full of powder? It looked just like my others. Why, it musta been one of them infantry rounds what got in my pouch by mistake. I wouldn't do a thing in this world to hurt ya. You know that."

"Do I?"

Frank stepped between them. "You hit the box, Johnny. Knocked a big ol' chunk out of the side of it."

"I did?" Johnny twisted around for a look.

"A' course you did," Kelley assured him. "Good shootin', too. Looks like you're about to get the hang of it."

Jim cackled. "Why, looky here, boys. I done found another bullet in my pocket. Reckon if Johnny here was real nice to me, I could let him have it fer his practicin'."

"Forget it!" Johnny grinned, his temper having died at the discovery of his marksmanship. "I'd let the Sioux scalp me before I'd take another shell from you."

"All right, Johnny," Kelley drawled, looking at his pocket watch. "Guard mount's in fifteen minutes, and if you're gonna have time to shoot your Colt, we better get at it."

The Scholar

^

JOHNNY SAT ON HIS BED watching the soldier four bunks down, who was known as the Scholar. The middle-aged man had curly, cottonlike white hair, dark eyes, and a smooth, chiseled face, which could easily have been a woman's.

He rarely spoke to anyone unless asked a question, and tonight he was doing what he always did before lights-out: reading. The shelf above his bunk was stacked high with books and old newspapers.

No one seemed to know anything about the Scholar, where he had come from or

what he was doing in the cavalry. Crazy Jim
had said he was once offered a promotion
to corporal but had refused it without giv-
ing a reason. One thing was known, the
man held a school teaching certificate and
was considered very knowledgeable by everyone in L Company.

The Scholar shifted his eyes from his
book to Johnny as if he knew he was being
watched. Johnny looked away, embarrassed
at having been caught staring. He had not
talked to the Scholar, but had been wanting
to. This might be as good an opportunity
as any. Most of the men in the barracks
were either gathered around a banjo player
at the far end of the room, singing, or
watching a cribbage game being played
near the stove.

Johnny walked to the foot of the Scholar's bed. "I'm sorry to bother you. Didn't
mean to stare. I was hoping maybe we
could visit some. If you're too busy, I
understand."

The Scholar marked his page with a
piece of red cloth, closed the book, and
swung his feet to the floor. "I'm not busy.

To tell you the truth, I was finding my eleventh reading of Mr. Shakespeare to be rather boring."

He held out his hand. "We haven't formally met, have we? Your name's Johnny, isn't it? Johnny McBane?"

"Yes, sir." Johnny shook hands.

The Scholar moved over a little to make room for Johnny. "Have a seat and tell me what's on your mind."

Johnny sat down, unsure what to say or where to begin. Ever since Crazy Jim had talked about the Sioux reservation in the Black Hills and the miners trespassing on it, Johnny's thoughts had been troubled. It didn't seem right for the Indians to have to stay on their reservation while white men were allowed to go there and dig for gold.

As the month of May and the time for the Seventh Cavalry's departure to fight the Sioux drew closer, the turmoil inside Johnny grew. He needed someone to talk to, someone who could explain what he longed to know.

Corporal Kelley, Crazy Jim, and a few of the others who had become his friends wouldn't understand his feelings. They would take them as a sign of weakness. And Frank didn't know any more about the Indians than Johnny did. The Scholar was his only hope.

Johnny kept his voice low, just loud enough for the Scholar to hear him. "Trouble is, I don't know what to think." He wanted to speak plainly, but decided against it. For all he knew the Scholar hated Indians and wished they were all dead.

"If...," Johnny tried framing his question carefully, "if you owned a house and someone else moved into it, and you tried to get them to leave but they wouldn't, would that make you mad?"

"Yes, I think so."

"Would you be mad enough about it to fight those people, or even to kill them, if that was the only way you had to get them to leave?"

"Maybe." The Scholar smiled. "That would depend on how much value I placed on the house and what my chances were of winning the fight. The house is no good to me if I'm dead, and in the case of the

Indians, to whom I believe you are refer-
ring, they have no chance. They may win
a battle here and there, but they will eventually lose the war. It is a certainty."

Johnny was silent a moment, amazed at
how quickly the Scholar had figured out the
true meaning of his question. "But...but
just because we're able to beat the Sioux
and take their land, does that make it
right?"

"No, but I'm afraid it is inevitable. Have
you ever heard the term *manifest destiny*?"

Johnny shook his head.

"Manifest destiny implies that a young
nation such as the United States has the di-
vine right, the God-given right, to expand
its territory for the development and wel-
fare of its people.

"There were some in our government
who used the phrase during the Mexican
War when we took Texas, California, and
most of what lay between away from Mex-
ico in the late forties. It was used when we
wrangled the Oregon country from Britain
and again by Southerners who wanted to

expand slaveholding rights to every state in the Union. The term is now being used to justify the taking of more Indian land."

Johnny shifted his weight on the bunk, twisting to better face the Scholar. "Does this manifest destiny make what we do right? Why do we have to put the Sioux on a reservation? What's wrong with just letting them go wherever they want and the whites can do the same?"

"The answer to your first question is no. Manifest destiny has not and cannot justify anything except in the eyes of those who believe in it, which happens to be a fairly large segment of our population. The answers to your other questions are not that simple.

"The Sioux are but one of more than a hundred Indian tribes in the United States. Most of the smaller ones, especially those in the East, have already been crushed. Right now there are ten whites in the West for every Indian. The Plains Indians—the Sioux, Cheyenne, Arapaho, Kiowa, and Comanche—claim thousands of square

miles of land, land that white settlers, trappers, traders, and miners want, and are will-
ing to kill to get.

"If the government doesn't establish reservations and force the Indians to live on
them, the American Indian will become ex-
tinct. He will be wiped off the face of this
country like chalk is wiped from a slate."

Johnny frowned and the Scholar went
on to explain, his voice becoming firmer.
"Look, I understand what is going through
your mind. I have spent considerable time
wrestling with questions like yours myself,
but you are going to have to quit looking
at the right and wrong of these issues.

"The fact is that thousands of people are
pouring into the West every day. These
people want the land, and no Indian is going to stop them from getting it. Unless the
army is able to put the Indian on a reservation and keep him there, the sheer num-
bers of our population will eventually grind
him to powder."

The banjo player and singers stopped,
and Johnny looked around to see if anyone
was listening before speaking. "Are you say-

ing we are doing the Indians a favor by taking their land and forcing them to live on
reservations?"

"No, of course not. What I am saying is
that from the government's point of view,
there is no other solution."

Johnny looked between his knees at the
floor. Though the Scholar had told him to
get past the issue of right and wrong, he
couldn't.

Following an uncomfortable moment of
silence, Johnny raised his head. "None of
what you've said explains why the government lets people go on the Sioux reservation to do whatever they want, when the
Indians aren't allowed off of it."

"Greed is the reason, and power. The
treaty of 1868 unmistakably established the
Black Hills for the Sioux, but rumors of
gold, and cool, flowing streams, and fertile
farmland have caused the whites to want
the land. This isn't the first time the government has cheated the Indian, and I doubt it
will be the last. We take what we want because we can."

Seeing the despondent look on Johnny's

face, the Scholar softened his tone. "Perhaps someday you and I will be in a position to dictate justice, to decide what is fair and equitable. For now, we must live under the decisions and directions made by others. They are out of our control."

Johnny nodded and rose from the bunk. If nothing else, the Scholar's last statement had solved his worst dilemma. There was nothing he could do about any of it.

"Thanks," Johnny said. "You've helped a lot. Maybe I'll quit thinking about it so much."

"Fine, Johnny. If you need to talk again, I'm here."

The door to the barracks opened, and Corporal Kelley came inside, followed by another man. "We got a new recruit, boys," Kelley said. "This here is Ben Hailey."

A few of the soldiers nodded a greeting. Hailey didn't seem to notice, nor did the grim expression change on his fleshy, heavy-boned face. Kelley led him past the stove to the end of the room, where Johnny's and Frank's beds were.

Kelley indicated an empty bunk beside

Frank's. "This will be yours. Make yourself at home. I'll go over to supply and see if I can round you up a couple of blankets."

The corporal left, and Johnny headed toward his bed. As he approached it, he saw the new recruit swing the flour sack holding his possessions on top of Frank's legs. Frank, who was lying down, sat up. "What do you think you're doing?"

"Get out," Hailey said dryly.

Frank kicked the sack to the side, sending it to the floor with a loud thud. He gestured at the empty bunk with the straw mattress rolled up at the head. "Corporal said that one there is your bunk."

"I like yours better," Hailey sneered. "Get your stuff and move out."

Frank quickly slid off his bed and jumped to his feet, his face just inches from Hailey's. "Won't be that easy, mister. I don't know where you come from or who you think you are, but I ain't goin' nowhere."

Johnny stood still, apprehension flooding through him. His muscles tightened. Hailey was obviously mean and sure of himself. But more than that, Johnny sensed he was dangerous. In the saloons and brothels of Chicago there had been dozens of men like Hailey, men who had something to prove, who almost never fought fair, and who had few qualms, if any, when it came to killing.

The room grew quiet, and it was all Johnny could do to keep from butting in. He knew Frank would be angry with him if he did. The trouble did not involve him, and with every soldier in the room watching, Frank's pride was at stake.

Hailey started to unbutton his coat in a deliberate, threatening way. He was down to his last button when Corporal Kelley came in with the blankets.

"Taps hasn't been played yet. Why's everybody so quiet?"

No one answered and Kelley walked down the aisle, stopping beside Johnny. "What's goin' on?"

"Your new man wants Frank's bunk," Johnny replied coldly.

Kelley handed the blankets to Johnny. "What's wrong with you, Hailey? I told you what bunk was yours. We don't put up with troublemakers here in L Company. There's a couple of empty bunks down by the door where the wind will hit you every time the door is opened. Take one of those or find yourself another place to live."

Hailey opened his coat, purposely exposing a pistol tucked in his waistband.

"That gun don't scare me," Kelley declared. "We got a hundred of 'em. All I have to do is say the word and every soldier here will be all over you. You'll be tied up and in the guardhouse before you know what's happened."

He jerked his thumb toward the other end of the room. "Now get your blankets and go on to your bunk, and I won't say nothing about this to the sergeant. Any more trouble out of you and I will."

Hailey reached down and picked up the sack Frank had knocked to the floor. He brushed past Kelley. Over his shoulder he sneered, "I'll be seeing you again. Be watching."

Town

$\wedge$

YOU EVER GOIN' TO get through pol-
ishin' your boots? They're just gonna
get muddy, and Bismarck'll be closed down
before we ever get there."

Johnny grinned. It hadn't been an hour
since L Company had been given a furlough
into town, and Frank had not stopped pac-
ing for at least half that long.

"Almost ready, Frank," Johnny said. "I
told you to go on without me."

"Nope. It's Saturday night and our first
trip to town since we got here. We're goin'

in together, *if* you're able to get your coat on before tomorrow mornin'."

Johnny shoved the polish rag back in the cleaning kit, put the kit in his footlocker, then checked his shirt pocket to be sure his money was still there. Except for his laundry, which he paid one of the women on Suds Row to do, there was little to spend money on. He had close to twenty dollars.

Frank impatiently moved to the wall and took Johnny's coat off a peg. "Here. I know you can do it. Just put one arm in this sleeve and then the other'n in this one."

The two left the barracks and started walking on the road leading to Bismarck. It was nearly the middle of May, and though a good while remained before dusk, dark, threatening rain clouds hid the sun.

On the top of a short swell, Johnny stopped and gazed back at Fort Lincoln. Beyond it, down on the Missouri River flats, a city of tents had been built to hold the recent influx of troops. All twelve

companies of the Seventh Cavalry had arrived, along with two companies of the Seven-
teenth Infantry and one company of the
Sixth. Johnny had heard that, counting everyone, there were nearly a thousand men.

The scene reminded him of why the
troops were here and what lay ahead. Lieutenant Colonel George Armstrong Custer
had arrived at Fort Lincoln, resuming command from Major Reno, and in less than a
week the Seventh would be going out after
the Sioux.

Johnny had seen Custer only once, and
then at a distance, but it was enough to
confirm the image he had long held.
Mounted on a big, powerful gray horse and
dressed in fringed buckskins, Custer looked
every bit the dashing frontier Indian fighter
and big-game hunter Johnny had heard
about.

"Hey," Frank yelled. "I didn't know you
was so fond of the fort that you couldn't
stand to leave. It'll be there when we get
back. Come on. We're gonna miss the
fun."

Johnny trotted to catch up with his friend. By the time they reached Bismarck, the street lamps had been lit and the town was bustling. People, buggies, wagons, and riders lined the muddy main road. Frank and Johnny stayed to the side, where boardwalks had been built in front of some of the establishments. The sound of a woman's singing, accompanied by a piano, came from somewhere ahead.

Frank's pace quickened. He reached the door where the music was coming from and motioned for Johnny to hurry up. "Let's go in here. I'll buy you a beer."

"No, thanks. I never could get used to the taste of the stuff." He touched the back of his head. "You go ahead. I haven't had a haircut in months, and I want to look around town some, maybe find a barber who's still open. I'll come back by later."

"You sure? There's prob'ly some purty girls dancin' around in there."

"Go on. I won't be long."

"All right. Guess there's no changin' your mind." Frank smiled broadly and

opened the door. "Here I go. I'll be lookin'
for ya."

∧

SOMETIME LATER Johnny returned. He had
gotten a haircut and bought a used pocket
watch and a small leather coin purse from
a street trader for a dollar. He'd also bought
an imitation-pearl-handled penknife at a
mercantile store for two bits and eaten a
heaping plate of fried chicken at a café,
which was a welcome change from army
chow.

Johnny stepped up on the plank walk in
front of the saloon where he had left Frank.
A drunk lay in his path, and he stepped over
him, briefly reminded of Chicago and the
dozens of winos who lined the streets there
every night.

As he walked inside, the strong stench
of cigar smoke and whiskey hit him. The
room was large and dimly lit. Again he was
reminded of Chicago and the barroom life
he'd left behind. He was glad he had come
west—glad *that* part of his life was over.

Several men were standing by a long bar

at the far end of the room, a couple of them wearing military uniforms. To their left were rows of crowded tables, and above them a woman stood on a curtainless stage, singing.

Johnny went to the bar. Frank wasn't there, but Sergeant O'Connell was. O'Connell glanced at him with red, puffy eyes, then downed a shot glass full of whiskey. "Well, if it ain't Private McBane, the biggest liar at Fort Lincoln."

Johnny warily took a step back. Whether the liquor was doing the talking or the sergeant really meant what he had said, Johnny couldn't tell. Either way, he didn't want any trouble if it could be avoided.

"I was looking for Private Gann, sir. Have you seen him?"

O'Connell inclined his head toward the stage. "He's over there somewhere, playin' cards."

"Thanks." Johnny started for the tables.

"McBane!" O'Connell barked.

Reluctantly, Johnny stopped and turned around.

"The name Julian Dean mean anything to you?"

The sergeant saw Johnny's stunned look and did not wait for an answer. "Sure it does. I told you I'd do some checking." He reached in his back pocket and took out a folded letter. "This just came in. Dean says you owe him some money. He also says you are not old enough to be in the army."

"Dean wouldn't know," Johnny replied testily. "He wasn't around when I was born, and if anybody owes money, it's him."

"Well, I'll see about that. I think you're lying, as usual."

Johnny wanted to tell O'Connell to think whatever he liked, but he held his tongue, turned, and hurriedly made his way through the maze of tables to get away and look for Frank. However it had happened, apparently Dean had found out where he was, and that bothered Johnny far more than the sergeant did. Still, Chicago was a long way off. The question was, *was it far enough?*

Johnny finally found Frank sitting at a

corner table away from the stage, playing blackjack with Corporal Kelley and Crazy Jim. A chair to the side was empty, so he sat down.

"Hey, Johnny," Frank said loudly, his slurred speech exposing his drunkenness. "Look." He grabbed some of the money in front of him and let it fall through his fingers. "I'm winnin'. Here." He threw a bill in front of Johnny. "Buy yourself a beer."

Johnny glanced at Kelley and Jim, neither of whom looked too happy. "No, Frank, I told you I don't like the stuff. I'm going on back to the fort. You about ready to go with me?"

"Naw." Frank swung his arm, accidentally knocking a near-full glass off the table. It hit the wooden floor and broke, drawing the attention of everyone around. "I ain't goin' nowhere."

Frank paused, took a deep breath, and grinned. "These two polecats got some more money, and I'm gonna take it off 'em. Tonight's my lucky night."

Johnny bent over and picked up the broken glass. As he sat up, a figure suddenly loomed behind Frank. Johnny recognized him instantly. It was Ben Hailey, the recruit who had tried to take Frank's bunk a few weeks ago. Corporal Kelley had had more trouble with him the next day and had managed to get him transferred to another company. Johnny hadn't seen him since.

"Not anymore," Hailey taunted. "I'm takin' your place."

Corporal Kelley leaned back in his chair. "Leave Gann alone. Is that all you got to do, go around trying to stir up trouble? This is a private game, and me and Jim want a chance to win our money back."

"It don't matter what you want. We're not at Fort Lincoln now, and them two stripes on your arm don't mean nothin' to me."

"You're wrong about that. I outrank you no matter where we're at."

Hailey ignored Kelley's remark, placing his elbow on the table and leaning down so that his face was close to Frank's.

"*Move.*"

Frank was still smiling in a flushed stupor, looking as if he didn't have a care in the world. "I don't like you," he declared. "Why don't you go stick your head in a slop bucket?"

Hailey reacted in a blur, knocking Frank's hat off, grabbing his hair, and jerking him backward so that he and his chair went crashing to the floor.

Then he kicked him.

Johnny jumped up. Frank was too drunk to defend himself. Using the table for support, Johnny vigorously swung his body around the edge, planting the soles of both boots full in Hailey's chest. Hailey flew back into another table, smashing it and sending the men seated there sprawling.

Crazy Jim and Corporal Kelley helped Johnny raise Frank to his feet. Johnny glanced to the side. Hailey was getting up, and he was reaching under the front of his coat, possibly for his pistol.

The saloon was now quiet. Sergeant O'Connell's footsteps were loud on the wooden floor. "What's the trouble here, Kelley?"

Kelley pointed at Hailey, whose hands now hung by his sides, empty. "He started it. We were just playing cards when he grabbed hold of Gann and threw him on the floor and went to kicking him. Johnny here—I mean Private McBane—put a stop to that quick enough."

O'Connell looked at Hailey only briefly before focusing his full attention on Johnny. The look in his eye seemed to take on a kind of mocking amusement. "So you like to fight, do you? Maybe you think you're pretty good at it. Maybe you'd like to try *me*?"

"No, Sarge," Kelley blurted. "I told you, Johnny didn't do anything wrong. It was all Hailey."

"You're out of line, Kelley," O'Connell snapped, keeping his eyes on Johnny. "I'm in charge here.

"What about it, McBane? You too yellow to step out back with me? It won't take long."

Johnny's heart raced. His breaths were short. It wasn't right what O'Connell was doing, wasn't right that Hailey got off free. The sergeant at Jefferson Barracks had not been right, either, and Johnny could no longer contain his outrage—nor did he want to.

He swung. The power in his right arm brought him to his toes as the blow caught O'Connell squarely on the chin.

The sergeant staggered backward.

Johnny suddenly felt free. He eagerly plowed into the sergeant's middle with both fists. Now he was the one in charge, doing the one thing he knew he was good at.

The sergeant continued to back away, knocking over the poker table where Frank, Crazy Jim, and Kelley had been playing, until he was in the corner and could go no further. Johnny refused to let up, and in a desperate attempt to stop the fiery onslaught, O'Connell covered his head with his arms and charged like a bull.

Johnny hit him once more, aiming at an unprotected patch of hair, then leaped sideways. His left foot landed on a small brass spittoon, twisting his ankle and causing him to lose his balance.

Johnny fell to the floor.

O'Connell saw his chance. With blood

streaming from his nose and mouth, he swung a chair over his head and started for Johnny.

Crazy Jim grabbed one of the chair legs. "No, ya ain't. Turn loose. The kid's beatin' ya fair."

The time Jim gave Johnny was enough. He was on his feet and coming. Having no choice, O'Connell released his hold on the chair and put up his fists, but his earlier sureness was gone. There was doubt in his eyes. Johnny could see it.

Johnny didn't hesitate. He drove into him like a whirlwind, throwing a savage fusillade of punches. The sergeant tried to fight back, but his efforts only hurt his defense, making his face and stomach more vulnerable.

O'Connell was weakening. Despite the man's hot, unrestrained rage, Johnny could sense it, and the knowledge caused him to fight harder still.

Johnny's hands were bruised and torn, perspiration stung his eyes, and his lungs burned for lack of air, yet he ignored all of it.

The sergeant wearily dropped his arms, ending all resistance, and Johnny knew it was nearly over.

He took a step back, gathered his weight, and let go with a roundhouse right. The blow clapped against O'Connell's jaw, and the man stumbled, then dropped.

Johnny used his sleeve to wipe his sweaty face. He looked around. "Where's Hailey?"

"He's done left." Crazy Jim beamed. "He seen enough to know he don't want none of ya."

The sergeant groaned, drawing Johnny's attention. He had made it to his hands and knees and was attempting to stand. By the time he finally made it to his feet, Johnny's anger was waning and foreboding was fast taking its place.

What would happen to him for what he had done? A court-martial, months in the guardhouse, or maybe even prison at Fort Leavenworth?

O'Connell spit blood on the floor, then took his finger and wiped out a piece of broken tooth. His nose looked as if it might be broken and his eyes were swollen.

He wobbled closer to Johnny and spoke between hard, ragged breaths. "Nobody's... ever... done this to me... and I've fought plenty... I didn't get a single lick in, did I?"

Johnny was surprised by the sergeant's calm voice. If he was upset, he hid it well. "You probably did. I'll know for sure when I wake up in the morning."

"Kelley," O'Connell barked. "You and McBane here help me to the bar." The corporal took hold of one arm, and Johnny the other. The sergeant raised his hands. "Listen, everybody. Belly up. Drinks are on me."

Johnny's anxiety faded. In its place was a touch of admiration. Any man who could take the beating O'Connell had and not want revenge was something.

Frank, Crazy Jim, Kelley, Johnny, and O'Connell lined up at the bar. The sergeant wiped his face with a wet bar towel, downed half a glass of beer in one swallow, then turned to Johnny.

"Where'd you learn to fight like that,

kid? You ripped me apart. I never had a chance."

"Chicago," Johnny answered softly. "Julian Dean was my manager."

"Aye." O'Connell smiled. "I see." He put the beer glass to his busted lips like he was going to drink, then set it down as if something important had dawned on him. "Listen, kid. I've fought some of the toughest around here, and none of them can touch me.

"You're the best and you're wasting it. When we get back from this expedition, we'll set up a few bouts—make a little money. As soon as you get known, we'll make more money. Lots of it. What do you say? A month's wages for a few minutes' work sounds good, doesn't it?"

Johnny shrugged. "Maybe. We'll see." The talk reminded him of the first time he had met Julian Dean.

"Sure it does." O'Connell picked up his glass again. "Johnny 'the Kid' McBane," he half whispered to himself. "Against any and all takers."

A Premonition

^

JOHNNY STOOD on the outskirts of the tent city below Fort Lincoln. Two days ago, he and Frank had transferred their gear into a tent, as everyone else had done.

He was on guard duty. His Colt revolver hung at his side, and the butt of his carbine was in his left hand, the barrel resting lightly against his shoulder.

Another guard who was slowly circling the camp approached him.

"Is that you, Private McBane?"

"Yeah," Johnny answered, recognizing

killed anyone. Don't want to kill anyone."

"It isn't wrong to feel like that, Johnny. In fact, I'd be disturbed if you felt any other way. Tell me something. I heard about your fight with Sergeant O'Connell in town. Did you go there with the intention of fighting or hurting him?"

"No. I didn't want to fight him, or Hailey, or anybody. Frank was drunk and in trouble and . . . and I got mad. It just happened."

"Then go on this campaign trip in the same frame of mind as when you went to Bismarck. If there comes a time when you must fight for yourself or your comrades, a time when you have no choice except to kill or be killed, you will know it."

"I hope you're right," Johnny answered, his voice barely above a whisper.

The Scholar was silent a moment. "There is something else you must understand. Regardless of their reasons for joining the military, all the men in this camp have one thing in common. They are soldiers.

"Their job, my job, your job is to serve our country by following orders whether we agree with them or not. A soldier's life is not his own; it belongs to his country."

"I think I understand. An army wouldn't be of much use if the soldiers in it didn't do what they were told."

"Exactly. When we get back I have some books I'd like for you to read. I think you could acquire a lot of useful information from them."

"Uh, I . . . I never went to school."

"I'll teach you to read, Johnny. It won't be difficult. You have a sharp, inquisitive mind. It would be a shame to waste it."

The Scholar looked over his shoulder at the lights of the huge camp. "I had better be getting back to my rounds." He started walking. "We'll talk more later."

A wolf howled somewhere in the distance. Johnny paid the lonely, mournful sound no mind. His thoughts were on the stacks of books and old newspapers above the Scholar's bunk. He wanted to read them, wanted to know all the things the Scholar knew.

A horse and rider appeared near the

fringe of the camp, reminding Johnny of the big-boned dun gelding Sergeant O'Connell had assigned him for the trip. According to Crazy Jim, the horse was a good one, and the sergeant had gone to considerable trouble to make sure Johnny got him. Johnny was glad Corporal Kelley had kept his promise and taught him how to ride, at least well enough to stay in the saddle.

The change in O'Connell since their fight in the Bismarck saloon was astonishing. Although Johnny appreciated the change, he did not trust it. Dean had been nice to him, too, at first. O'Connell was friendly, said nothing more about Johnny's age, and had ordered Corporal Kelley to personally inspect Johnny's campaign gear.

The items included two blankets plus a rubber ground cloth, a two-piece mess kit, a knapsack, half of a "dog tent," extra clothes, one hundred carbine rounds and twenty-four shells for his pistol, four days' salt pork and hardtack pack rations, an overcoat, a canteen, and ten pounds of grain for his horse.

A faint noise behind Johnny interrupted his thoughts. He turned to see a figure advancing in the gloom.

"Stop! Who's there?"

"Just me."

Johnny recognized Frank's voice, detecting a note of sadness in it. "What are you doing up?"

"Aw, I can't sleep. Somethin' don't feel right. I can't tell you what it is, 'cause I don't know myself, but there's somethin' I got to tell you.

"My...my name's not Frank Gann. I got that out of a newspaper. It's Horace, Horace Walker, and I ain't but nineteen. My folks wouldn't sign the papers for me to enlist, so I run off."

Frank took a deep breath. "If...if somethin' was to happen to me, I want you to get word to 'em. They're in Kentucky, not far out of Perryville. If I got any pay comin', see that it gets to 'em."

"Nothing's going to happen to you," Johnny said reassuringly. "We're going to see a lot of new places, have some fun, and before you know it, we'll be right back here."

Frank reached into his coat pocket, took out a folded letter, and handed it to Johnny. "You're the best friend I ever had. I mean that. See that they get that, too."

Johnny stared at the letter in his hand, trying to think of something to say. He looked up in time to see Frank silently disappear into the darkness. The wolf howled again. This time the mournful sound sent shivers down Johnny's spine.

Indians

^

THE NOON SUN was bright and the June day hot. Choking clouds of dust kicked up by the long column of horses in front of Johnny hung thick in the still air. The incessant rattle of equipment and the clatter of horses' hooves made it difficult to hear anything else.

Johnny shifted his weight in the saddle, allowed the sweat-lathered dun beneath him a little more slack in the reins, and reached for his canteen.

Five and a half long weeks had passed since the Seventh Cavalry had left Fort Lincoln. Except for being so saddle sore he could hardly move, Johnny had found the first few days of the trip exciting. He'd seen a distant herd of buffalo, several bunches of antelope, a few deer, and more wild back-country than he had thought existed in the whole world.

But life on the trail had quickly lost its glamour. A freak snowstorm had hit a little over a week out from the post, making several days and nights miserably cold and wet. And then it had hailed, followed by a steady rain, which it seemed would never stop. Now it was hot, stifling hot, and the sweaty flannel shirt on Johnny's back trapped the heat like an oven.

Johnny remembered the last and only time he'd had the chance to bathe since leaving the fort. That day had been cool, and the water in the Yellowstone River cold. He and Frank had hurriedly scrubbed their bodies with a bar of lye soap Corporal Kelley had loaned them. Johnny wished he was in that water now. He wished he could lie in it for a week—and sleep.

Sleep. Johnny closed his red, tired eyes a

moment. No one in the Seventh was getting more than a few hours of it a day. And last night, believing they were nearing the Sioux village, Colonel Custer ordered the troops roused from their blankets at midnight. Except for a break this morning barely long enough to brew coffee, the column hadn't stopped moving.

Johnny knew why Custer was in such a hurry. Everyone did. Several days ago the command had come across the corpse of an Indian. The body lay on a scaffold, and the posts supporting it were painted red and black. Crazy Jim said the paint meant the warrior had been unusually brave. Custer ordered the scaffold pulled down, and he and the other officers helped themselves to the dead man's clothing, bow and arrows, and rawhide bags. Then the stripped corpse was thrown into the river.

Not long after that, the column discovered a fresh Indian trail along the Rosebud Creek. The trail was a mile wide in places, and the grassy sod was churned to powder by the furrows of thousands of travois poles.

And then yesterday they had come upon the fresh scalp of a white man mounted on a stick and the remains of a huge Indian camp. Still standing was the frame of a dance lodge, which had a tall pole in the center of it surrounded by a pile of buffalo skulls.

That night, over a meal of salt pork and hardtack, Sergeant O'Connell had explained to Johnny and Frank all about the sun dance the Sioux had probably held in the lodge. The center pole was used to hold one end of an array of buffalo-hair and rawhide lariats. Both sides of the warriors' chests were cut by a medicine man, and sticks placed through the muscles.

The lariats were then attached to the sticks and tightened until the warrior's chest muscles were pulled and he was forced to stand on his toes. Sometimes, to make it more painful, the sticks were pushed through the dancer's cheeks just beneath the eyes or through the back muscles.

Hooked tightly to the pole, the warriors would dance for hours, sometimes days, until they tore their flesh loose from the sticks. If one of them cried out or fainted from the self-imposed torture, he would be treated like a squaw for the rest of his life. He would build lodges, carry firewood and water, tan hides, and help with the cooking. Even the women and children he was forced to stay with would have little to do with him. The sun dance was held once each summer to honor the sun, test the warriors' bravery and fortitude, and gain help from the spirit world.

From talk around the campfires Johnny had learned other things about the Sioux and their longtime chief, Sitting Bull. At the age of fifteen, Sitting Bull had distinguished himself by killing a Crow Indian and taking the scalp. That same year, in a fight with Flathead Indians, he had bravely galloped his horse in front of them, taking a foot wound.

Several years and many battles later, Sitting Bull became a tribal chief and a prophet, a holy man who received dreams and visions from Wakantanka, a god the Sioux described as the Great Mystery. Because of his bravery, his spiritual leadership, and his stubborn, lifelong opposition to the encroachment of whites on Sioux land, Sitting Bull had been elected head war chief of the entire Sioux Nation.

Johnny wondered what the great warrior looked like, then realized with a shock that he might soon find out. According to O'Connell, the trail they had found was made by the people of Sitting Bull's village.

An unintelligible shout came from ahead, and Johnny saw several companies split off to the left from the main column. The weary dun began to trot, as did all the horses, and the uneasy feeling that had been with Johnny since yesterday grew stronger.

Frank, who had been riding behind, spurred his horse alongside Johnny's. "This is it," he half yelled. "I know it. Custer's done found the village, and we're headin' for it."

Johnny was about to speak when the whole column broke into a hard gallop. Some distance farther they topped a cactus-and-sage-spotted bluff. Below lay a long, broad valley filled with so many tepees that the floor of it looked like a solid sheet of white.

The column slowed a little, and through the thick haze of dust Johnny could see Custer waving his hat and shouting. Surprisingly, the famous man's words were clear.

"Hold your horses, boys. There are plenty of them down there for all of us."

Johnny tightened his rein on the dun. Minutes later shots rang out below and he saw a cloud of dust form at the southern end of the village. He guessed that the men who had split from the column earlier were now down there, fighting.

The command swung to the right, dropping into a long ravine. At the bottom they entered a large, empty flat, and Johnny could see hundreds of Indians stretched out low on their ponies, racing toward them.

Guns boomed and roared. Piercing screams and yells seemed to come from everywhere. A soldier near the head of the column fell from his horse. Then another. Arrows whizzed past, striking the ground all around.

Frank reined his horse beside Johnny. His eyes were wide as he wildly gestured to the left. "Look! There's more injuns over there. There must be a thousand of 'em."

The air smelled of burnt gunpowder, and the thunder of gunfire grew louder. Johnny looked back. More Indians were coming from that direction. The column was scattering like a frightened covey of quail.

Johnny's thoughts raced. He had hoped this day, this moment, would never come. The Scholar's words echoed in his head. *If there comes a time when you must fight for yourself or your comrades, a time when you have no choice except to kill or be killed, you will know it.*

He reached for the Colt in his holster. A bullet whined past his forehead. He glanced to the side and saw Frank holding his throat and falling from his horse. The bullet that had almost killed him had hit his friend.

Johnny leaped from the dun, landing in a sprawling roll that knocked part of the wind out of him. He dodged the hooves of a horse and scrambled back to where Frank lay. His friend's lifeless blue eyes stared blankly at the sky. Blood covered his neck and chest.

Johnny stood up, raising the Colt in his hand. Through the blinding dust and gun smoke he saw a painted warrior clad only in a breechcloth bending over the body of a soldier.

He pulled back the hammer on the Colt and took aim.

An arrow hit Johnny deep in the chest, knocking him down. He shook his head, trying to stop the waves of darkness from blocking his sight.

He clutched his chest and gasped for air. Familiar sounds filled his head. The Chicago gambling crowd at The Store was chanting his name. In their chants he found strength.

Johnny rose to his knees.

Epilogue

^

ON MAY 17, 1876, to the tune of "Garry Owen" and under the command of General Alfred Terry, Lieutenant Colonel George Armstrong Custer led the Seventh Cavalry toward the Yellowstone River.

In mid-June, the Hunkpapa Sioux held a sun dance along Rosebud Creek, where Sitting Bull experienced a vision of many soldiers "falling right into our camp." The dead soldiers, he said, were gifts from God.

Not long thereafter, Sitting Bull's village more than doubled in size to an estimated

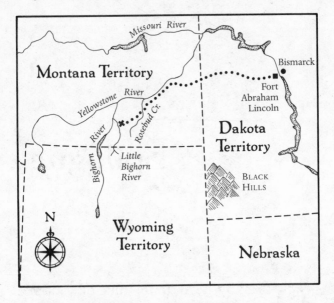

••• Custer and the Seventh Cavalry's route
     to the Battle of Little Bighorn

✖   Site of the Battle of Little Bighorn

1,000 lodges and 7,000 people, at least 2,000 of whom were warriors.

On Sunday, June 25, Custer located the enormous village along the Little Bighorn River and attacked it. The Indians fought with unusual unity and tenacity under the leadership of Gall, Crazy Horse, and others. Custer and the 215 cavalry men with him, companies C, E, F, I, and L, were killed. Three other companies under the command of Major Reno also suffered extensive losses and sound defeat.

Although the Battle of Little Bighorn was a tremendous triumph for Sitting Bull and his followers, it actually helped to hasten their demise. Americans, who were celebrating their nation's centennial, were stunned and horrified by news of the disaster. The people demanded revenge, and Congress responded by providing additional funds for more forts, recruits, training, and guns and ammunition.

Five years later, on July 19, 1881, after being driven to near starvation in Canada, Sitting Bull and 45 men, 67 women, and 73 children surrendered. When Sitting Bull handed over his gun at Fort Buford he said, "I wish it to be remembered that I was the last man of my tribe to surrender my rifle, and this day have given it to you."

Bibliography

^

Connell, Evan S. *Son of the Morning Star: Custer and the Little Bighorn.* New York: Promontory Press, 1993.

Rickey, Don Jr. *Forty Miles a Day on Beans and Hay.* Norman, Okla.: Univ. of Oklahoma Press, 1963.

Utley, Robert M. *Frontier Regulars: The United States Army and the Indian, 1866–1891.* [Lincoln, Nebr.]: Univ. of Nebraska Press, Bison Books, 1984.

———. *Cavalier in Buckskin.* Norman, Okla.: Univ. of Oklahoma Press, 1988.

———. *The Lance and the Shield: The Life and Times of Sitting Bull.* New York: John Macrae / Henry Holt & Co., 1993.